T0065598

Previous books:

JUST PASSIN' THROUGH ... My life's journey

UNCLE BEN AND ME. ... A story

"MY SON, MY SON". ... A story based on a historical event.

"Ride, Cowboy, Ride"

Romance Blossoms and Danger Threatens
on the Pony Express Trail...

Gordon B. Rose

WESTBOW
PRESS®
A DIVISION OF THOMAS NELSON
& ZONDERVAN

Scripture taken from the King James Version of the Bible.

WestBow Press books may be ordered through booksellers or by contacting:

WestBow Press
A Division of Thomas Nelson & Zondervan
1663 Liberty Drive
Bloomington, IN 47403
www.westbowpress.com
1 (866) 928-1240

ISBN: 978-1-5127-5567-1 (sc)
ISBN: 978-1-5127-5566-4 (hc)
ISBN: 978-1-5127-5568-8 (e)

Library of Congress Control Number: 2016914586

Print information available on the last page.

WestBow Press rev. date: 9/23/2016

DEDICATION ...

This book is dedicated to **Billy Tate** -- a fourteen-year-old rider for the Pony Express. Billy was chased into the hills in Nevada Territory by the Paiute Indians in 1860. He took shelter behind rocks, but in his fight to save the mail as well as himself, he lost his life. His body was found riddled with several arrows. However ... he killed seven Indians in the process. Billy was not scalped, showing the Paiutes honored their enemies. In the nineteen months that the Pony Express was in existence, this was the *only* time the mail did not get through. I hope to meet Billy one day in heaven. I want to hear about that battle ...

A SPECIAL THANKS. ...

To my sweet wife, Star. For her encouragement, proof reading and comments, and allowing me the many hours at the computer while God developed this story! I can't imagine life without her ...

CONTENTS

INTRODUCTION

The idea of the Pony Express was an amazing plan in its day. What an undertaking ... to line up riders, horses, relay stations -- many which had to be built -- station keepers, food and water for horses; the same for riders at the "home" stations. It was 1,900 miles of very dangerous travel on horseback by mostly young teenage boys.

Over one hundred riders were employed by investors William H. Russell, Alexander Majors, and William B. Waddell, during the time of the Pony Express ... and around four-hundred horses. Can you imagine the story each rider would have to tell about their upbringing, perhaps a girlfriend, and experiences on the trail in the mid-1800s?

Tad Rawlings had two goals in life: to be the first rider on the Pony Express, and to marry Laura Prescott. But Patch Gaines had the same two goals... and he was a mean one.

There is *excitement* just ahead in "Ride, Cowboy, Ride."

RIDE, COWBOY, RIDE!

JIM WAGNER FINISHED HIS BREAKFAST and, as was his habit, went out to sit on the front porch a while before commencing his usual farming chores. Although there had been two days of hard rain in the area, this southern Dakota Territory morning was bright and sunny. As his eyes scanned the horizon, a little over a mile straight across the open fields from his farm something looked different -- and it was the missing boulders that usually outlined the sky just above John and Pat Rawlings' farm house.

Jim quickly hollered inside to his wife, Sadie, that he needed to ride over to the Rawlings' farm. He tore out to the barn, hitched up a horse to the wagon and headed over. He remembered telling John several times that it was a real gamble to have a farm house that close to the bottom of Boulder Cliff. John would always reply, "Those boulders have been up there for thousands of years and they'll be there for thousands more."

As Jim got closer to the Rawlings' farm, his worst fears were realized: massive boulders had broken loose in a landslide, rolling and tumbling down the sloping ground. ... and into the farm house. Over the years the base around those boulders had been eroding away, and the torrential rains of the previous two days caused the law of gravity to exert its power. The largest ones hit and crushed the very center

1

of the house, while others rolled and bounced on past the far side for another hundred yards or more. One wing of the house was the only part that had escaped being totally demolished ... and it was in there that Jim found four-year-old Tad Rawlings.

ONE LIFE SPARED. ...

Jim had to break a window out in order to get to Tad who was so glad to see his neighbor, but immediately began crying. Jim wedged himself through the window and tried to comfort Tad. When he stopped crying Jim found he couldn't open the door out of Tad's bedroom due to the total collapse of the main part of the house.

After Jim handed Tad out the window and lowered him carefully to the ground, he grabbed all the clothes he could find, climbed out the window, and put Tad and the clothes into the wagon. He told Tad to stay there, and then went and explored the wreckage. As he went around the circumference of the demolished dwelling, he could see but a hand that was Pat's, and a booted foot that was John's. It was obvious that they had died instantly. His main job right now, once he composed himself before going back to Tad ... which took several minutes ... was to get him back to their house, feed him, and then he and Sadie had to decide what to do.

Jim had the horse go at a slow pace back to the farm house. On the way he tried talking to a weeping boy who was now an orphan. Tad asked Jim, "How could God let my parents die when they were such good people?" Jim's answer was, "Sometimes bad things happen to good people. But now your parents are with God and are all right. They love you and miss you very much, and one day you will all be together again."

Fortunately, Jim and Sadie had met John Rawlings' brother and wife, Porter and Lucy Rawlings, when they were up here visiting from Tanner in Kansas Territory a couple of years ago. Tanner was a small town on the west side of the Missouri River, just across from St. Joseph, Missouri.

Communication over long distances in the middle 1800s was slow, as a telegraph sent all the way to Tanner from southern Dakota Territory had to be relayed in somewhat of a zig-zag pattern. Jim told Sadie he would go into town and send a telegraph message to John's brother about what had happened. He would tell Porter and Lucy that they would take care of the funeral here, and that a good attorney friend in town would care for all financial concerns. And then the big question: Would he and Lucy be able to take Tad into their home and raise him as if he were their own child? If that was okay, Jim said he and Tad would take a stagecoach to Tanner as soon as he heard back.

Well, Jim got a telegraph back from Porter. He told Jim that he and Lucy would be very happy to take Tad into their home, love him and raise him.

It was going to be a week before a stage would be leaving in a direction toward Tanner. Jim used this time to get his attorney friend to ride with him over to the Rawlings' demolished homestead and determine what needed to be done. As they viewed the devastation, they immediately knew that mankind would not be moving the main giant boulder that had completely crushed the main part of the house … and became the gravestone of this husband and wife.

JIM'S THOUGHT WAS TO GET some men to remove all the wood and debris they could, leaving Tad's room intact. They would come out about one hundred feet, build a low fence around the entire area, and erect a dated Memorial Plaque in honor of this Christian husband and wife. Pat's hand and Jim's foot would be covered, and then dirt landscaped around the boulder area. The farm acreage would just stay as it was, and perhaps when little Tad had grown up a portion of it could be sold for him to begin his own farm or ranch somewhere.

Jim's attorney agreed with that plan. As a close friend of the Rawlings, the attorney offered to take charge and see everything through to completion -- after first getting another telegrammed approval from Porter Rawlings.

MAY 10TH, 1843 ...

Jim got two stagecoach tickets for May 10, 1843, for Tad and him to eventually get to Tanner. Jim had been a very successful farmer; he had a good, reliable farmhand, and now that his children were grown and married, his years of frugal money management allowed Sadie and him to get away when they wanted to. Another neighbor about a quarter of a mile away would check on Sadie the three weeks or so that he would be gone.

AND SO, A FOUR-YEAR-OLD boy got his first taste of a ten-day bumpy stagecoach ride as it zigged and zagged on the way to Tanner ... and he loved it! And Porter and Lucy Rawlings got their first taste of a four-year-old "son". They had not been able to have children of their own. They already had a bedroom fixed up for Tad, and a few toys that every boy would like.

Jim spent the night with the Rawlings, and would catch a stage the very next morning to take him back up Dakota way. While Tad played in his room with his new toys, Jim shared in the grief with Porter and Lucy as he related in more detail about the tragedy that took the lives of a wonderful couple, but spared that of their little boy. In a way it was amazing that the boulders didn't touch Tad's bedroom. While they didn't understand God allowing the loss of Tad's parents, they thanked him for sparing their precious son.

It was after the prayer they had together that Porter thanked Jim for taking care of the task of cleaning up the devastation caused to the house, landscaping around the boulders and the graves they caused, and the memorial plaque. Then he asked one more favor of Jim ... to erect two crosses with John's and Pat's names on them since that would be their final resting place "until Jesus comes again" ... and lifts up that boulder!

It was a tearful goodbye as Jim got on the stage that next morning ... even for Tad. He had gotten to know Jim really well on their stagecoach ride down here. ... felt like he was a close relative.

A NEW LIFE FOR THREE RAWLINGS …

Porter and Lucy raised horses for a living on a spread a few miles off the beaten path to Tanner. Porter knew horses better 'n anyone else in that part of the mid-west, and he began to have exciting plans to bring Tad up in this happy, profitable, horse-loving environment. He felt this could well be God's answer to a thought that had been eating at him in recent years: Who would take his place and do the same first-class job he had been doing all his working life?

THE LONGER PORTER RAWLINGS was in the horse-raising business, the wiser he became on how to raise horses so they would be very healthy, and also calm around people. From the time a foal was born, Porter was around it so it got as used to seeing him as it did its own mother! He also got his wife around all the horses every day, and any one who visited the ranch. The horses grew up totally at ease around people.

The demand for quality horses was growing: Stagecoach companies didn't want horses that weren't tame and didn't have stamina; the United States Cavalry had need of top-quality stock; moms and dads on farms or ranches could reward a son or daughter at graduation, or a special birthday, with no greater gift than a healthy horse that was clearly people-friendly.

Even as a foal (a horse under one-year), Porter would lean on their backs off and on a little, and it became easier to eventually put a saddle on, and mount the horse ... simply because it had a trust in people.

As little Tad Rawlings grew up, he developed the same love for horses his uncle had, who had now become his "dad". When he wasn't being schooled by his "mom" he was helping dad with the chores around the ranch ... and lovin' it.

The stock of horses grew in number on the Rawlings' ranch, and Porter realized he needed to hire a ranch hand. He kept his eyes and ears opened whenever he was in town for just the right guy. He was looking for one who would be a good worker, who loved horses, and especially ... was absolutely trustworthy.

MONTY ...

Porter had stopped in the blacksmith's shop one Saturday afternoon, and accidentally bumped into a young man as he went out the door. They both apologized to each other, and began a friendly conversation. Turned out this guy, Monty, had just quit a job on a ranch in south-eastern Nebraska Territory because the owner was a dishonest person, and he didn't want to work for a man like that. He had his own horse, so Porter invited him out to his ranch for dinner that night. Under the circumstances he knew Lucy wouldn't mind.

That evening Porter, Lucy and Tad, who was now ten years old, got acquainted with Monty. It became evident that Monty had the same good character and values in life that the Rawlings had ... and were teaching Tad. And so Monty was asked to join the Rawlings' "team" full-time in raising top-quality horses.

WHEN TAD WAS ABOUT SIXTEEN years old, a small church was erected on the outskirts of Tanner. They were able to get a school teacher, Bonnie Binghamton, to come out from the east to use the building during the weekdays. The cost of the building as well as supporting a teacher meant that families had to pay a small amount for their kids to attend. Fortunately, Porter and Lucy could easily afford for Tad to take advantage of some formal schooling, relieving Lucy of that responsibility ... at least for a couple of years. It put an extra load on Porter and Monty when Tad was in school, but weekdays he was just gone for five or six hours, and then it was right back to the ranch and doing what he loved.

A neighbor of the Rawlings was falling on hard times financially, and was trying to sell off some of his livestock as well as a few horses he had. Porter wanted to do his neighbor a favor and bought one of the worst looking horses ... one that no normal buyer would take. Out of the goodness of his heart, Porter paid him more than the horse was actually worth. The horse's name was "Old Buster". He was actually a young horse, but his coat was patchy gray, and he just looked old. Instead of Tad riding one of the prize horses on the ranch to school and having it just stand in one place for five hours, Porter had Tad hook up a buckboard to Old Buster and let him pull him to school each day ... and some days he could then go into Tanner after school and pick up some groceries and supplies to bring back to the ranch.

One day when Porter and Lucy were visiting a friend whose husband had recently died, she wanted to give Porter the Stetson cowboy hat her husband had bought but hardly had the chance to wear before he suddenly died. It was a beautiful looking cowboy hat, but when Porter tried it on it was a little too small. The lady then suggested he see if Tad would like it. He thanked her for such a meaningful gift, and later that day presented it to Tad to see if it would fit and if he would like it. It fit, and he loved it ... wore it to school every day, unless it was raining, and then he wore an older hat. Tad really treasured that hat ... there was not a nicer cowboy hat that he had seen anywhere in town. Most men wore hats that showed their age because they took no pride in them.

Lucy made sure Tad had clean jeans and shirt each day to go to school. Too many of the kids didn't take any pride in their appearance and she felt Tad could be a good example to them, especially with his friendly personality. His shiny school cowboy boots were worn for that and that only ... no corral work with horses for those boots! And his favorite plaid shirt was one that he wore in both circumstances, so Lucy had a job washing that on a continual basis.

"MUMPS" AND "BB" ...

Tad's occasional trips into Tanner were noticed by a couple of guys who only had each other for friends; in view of their uncouth, brazen personalities it is easy to see why. They liked to razz Tad, calling him "Dude" because he looked so sharp. Tad asked some people who those two were, and they said "Mumps" and "BB". The big jowls on Mumps made it a natural nickname, but Tad had to ask how BB got those initials. The best guess was because he had a Big Belly. Someone thought it stood for Beer Belly, but they were never observed drinking even though they acted somewhat like they had. They'd been called those names for so long that no one remembered who came up with them. They said the best thing Tad could do was to ignore them. So Tad did ... except he always gave them a smile. They didn't know how to handle that! No one had ever smiled at these two before ... both of them looking like they hadn't washed their clothes in months. One day as Tad got on the buckboard seat in town and began to head back to the ranch, Mumps hollered, "Hey, Dude. Don't let Old Buster get away from you." ... and then he and BB laughed and laughed. Tad smiled at them ... and they stopped laughing.

WADE-BERRY ...

Monty and Porter were taking a break from ranch work one day, when Monty mentioned about a special feed that had seemed to enhance the appearance and general muscle tone of some horses at the ranch he had left. The owner, Randall Wade, happened to stumble on this fact as it was growing wild on his ranch ... and no place else that he knew of. The rancher kept it a secret. Monty left that ranch under good conditions, but he was still owed some money by Randall who asked him to come back later to pick it up. He talked to Porter about maybe he could ride up there and the owner would agree to giving him some of what he called "wade-berry", in place of the money he was owed. Porter was willing to give it a try, especially under Monty's recommendation, so Monty grabbed some burlap sacks, hooked a horse up to a small wagon, and headed up Nebraska way. Porter said he would pay Monty the salary his former boss owed him if this experiment worked out well for his horses.

Several days went by, and Monty got back to the Rawlings' ranch with some burgeoning sacks of wade-berry. He was able to dig them up with the root systems. Monty explained to Porter how they are fast growing, and spread out somewhat like a strawberry patch. The berries are rather sparse, but it is felt the benefits to a horse's system lies as much in the leaves as in the berries. It sends out underground rhizomes, and thereby proliferates quickly. Another advantage is that it gives off a slight, but detectable, sweet smell to humans ... perhaps even more-so to horses. Porter, Monty and Tad got these "starts" planted in early fall in a separate enclosed pasture, watered them profusely, and they began growing immediately. The next spring they really took off.

Porter was trying to think of a way to test this wade-berry and know if it was responsible for a horse's better health and appearance. He remembered a story back in the first chapter of the book of Daniel in the Bible, where Daniel and three of his friends were four of the captured Israelites who were taken to Babylon. Instead of the rich food and drink the king's people consumed, Daniel suggested that the four of them eat vegetables and drink water. And in ten days they were much healthier than the ones who ate the king's food. That sounded like a good idea to Porter as a way to make his own test about the validity of wade-berry for improving the health of horses. By late spring Porter reasoned it would be good to let four horses (after all, it was Daniel plus three of his friends!) into that pasture and see if they were drawn to the wade-berry, or if they had wasted their time and effort.

FOR SOME UNEXPLAINED REASON, some of the Rawlings' horses had white "stockings" on opposing front and rear legs ... right front and left rear. This contrasted beautifully with their dark brown coat. ("Stockings" come up almost to the knee of the horse. Shorter ones might be called "socks"). This alternate marking was an inherited trait that seemed peculiar to only some horses on the Rawlings' ranch. They were healthy horses, and one of them Tad named "Blitzen" ... his favorite. Another was his "backup" favorite, and Porter let him name him also. He chose "Donner".

After the horses were fed each day ... healthy feed plus hay ... Porter led four of them into the pasture which had the wade-berry to see if they were willing to top-off their meal on it or if they would ignore it. These four horses, including Blitzen and Donner, loved the new addition to their diet. After this daily routine of having the same four horses complete their feeding time with wade-berry for three months, there was a noticeable increase in muscle definition along with a brighter luster to their coats when compared to the rest of the stock. In order to let the wade-berry proliferate more in that small pasture, Porter waited until the next spring to include the entire stock of horses.

TAD WAS JUST SHY OF NINETEEN when he became the first graduate of Tanner School. Bonnie, the school-marm, was really happy to see her efforts pay off in Tad's graduation ... especially since he was such a good example to the younger kids in the one-room school who looked up to him.

LAURA ...

One day Tad's shirt sleeve caught on a fence post of the corral and
ripped. He liked that shirt and hoped his mom could sew it without
it looking repaired. But, one glance by his mom told her she could
never sew it without it showing even though the plaid design would
mask it somewhat. She suggested that Tad take it to "Molly's Sewing
and Repair Shop" in Tanner. Perhaps they could do a better job. Tad
hooked the buckboard up to Old Buster and headed into town. He
tied Old Buster to a hitching post and went into Molly's shop. Over
to the left, operating a treddle sewing machine, was the prettiest girl
he had seen in his life. Another lady in the shop, Molly, the owner,
said, "Welcome. Can I help you?" Tad didn't hear her, as his attention
was totally focused on the blonde seamstress who was not even aware
he was there. Molly cleared her throat and repeated herself but even
louder than the first time. Tad went up to Molly who introduced
herself, and he showed her the bad tear in the shirt he hoped she could
repair since it was his favorite shirt.

Molly called, "Laura, can you come here a minute?" Laura came
over and was shown the tear in the sleeve of Tad's shirt. Molly said she
needed to get back to completing some book work, so Laura looked
over the tear, while Tad looked over Laura! After looking carefully
at the zig-zag tear, Laura told Tad that mending it with needle and
thread would not leave a good appearance. She explained that because
the tear crossed over different colors in the plaid design, she would

need to change different color thread multiple times. However, there was a new technique she would like to try on it. It consisted of a patch of material that had an adhesive on the back that would stick to material when enough heat was applied. She said she could turn the sleeve inside-out, cut a piece of the patching material to the right size to cover the torn area, and iron it on after carefully bringing both sides of the torn section into proper alignment. Laura said she thought the tear would hardly be noticed when the sleeve was then turned right-side out, especially since it had a plaid pattern. Tad was real excited about that, and explained to Laura that this was his favorite shirt and it meant a lot to him. In trying to explain that to Laura, he stammered a bit as he was quite taken in by her appearance ... every bit a lady in a small cowboy-oriented town.

Trying to think of more things to talk about, Tad asked Laura if she had heard of the Rawlings' Ranch. She said she had and that she heard they raised the best horses in the mid-west. And ... that was all his blushing mind could think of to say, so he asked Laura when the shirt would be ready. She said the very next day. As Tad went out the door, he was already excited about coming back! About the time he got to Old Buster, he heard a guy holler out, "Hey!" Tad looked around and a young guy with a somewhat mean look on his face walked up to him and said, "What were you doing in there?"

"Just took a torn shirt in to have it repaired."

"Seems like it took you a long time," the guy said. Tad noticed the extra large belt buckle he wore that had the word "Patch" written on it.

Tad replied, "I don't think so. Why?"

"Remember one thing. ... Laura Prescott is *my* girl! Don't mess with her!" With that he spat in the dirt just in front of Tad's feet, and walked across the street.

RIDING ON THE BUCKBOARD behind Old Buster on the way back to the ranch, Tad began to feel some anger about the way this stranger talked to him. In the first place, as sweet as Laura was it seemed impossible she would be attracted to a guy like that. Maybe his mom or dad might know who the guy is.

When he got in the ranch house, he explained about leaving the shirt and what Laura was going to do to repair it. And then he told about his confrontation with this guy who had a large belt buckle with the word Patch on it. His dad immediately said, "Oh, that must have been Patch Gaines. Yes, he's a mean one. I would just stay away from him. He's got a bad reputation. His mom left his dad because he drank too much, and so he lives with an alcoholic father. I tried talking to his dad once about the bad example he was setting for his son … but he wouldn't listen to me."

Tad spent the afternoon working with several of the horses … putting a saddle on one, and riding around so the other horses would get used to seeing this on a daily basis … and then putting the saddle on another horse and doing the same thing. Then another … all the time thinking about the girl he had just met that morning, and would get to see again the next day. And hoping Patch Gaines would not be around this time.

TAD WAITED UNTIL AFTER LUNCH to head into Tanner … and Laura Prescott. As he walked in the door of the sewing shop, Laura saw him immediately and greeted him with a big smile which went in through his eyes and directly to his heart! She showed Tad the sleeve she had repaired, and, indeed, the repair would only be noticed if you knew it was there to start with and purposely looked for it. Tad was really pleased and asked Laura how much he owed her. She said that this was the first repair she had made that way, and that he needed to wear it a while to make sure it would last. If it was okay after a few days and a couple of washings, he could pay for it then. What a deal!

About that time another customer came into the shop, a middle-aged man, who immediately came over to Laura and greeted her ... and she, him. Tad could tell they were good friends. Laura introduced the gentleman to Tad: "Tad, I'd like you to meet Parson Millard. He is the pastor at Tanner Church on the edge of town." Tad said, "Very glad to meet you. I went to school in that building for a couple of years." To which the parson replied, "I'm glad to make your acquaintance, Tad ... and invite you to visit our church some Sunday morning."

Laura spoke up and said, "Why don't you come this Sunday, Tad? I go there every Sunday with my aunt and uncle ... Aunt Molly and Uncle Kyle. It's a nice church with very friendly people. My aunt and uncle have raised me since I was six. My parents died in a fire at our house one weekend. Fortunately I was staying with my aunt and uncle that weekend or I wouldn't be here now." Her eyes dropped to the floor for a second as a tinge of sadness arose in her heart. "However, I know they are in heaven and that we will be together again one day." ... and a smile arose on her face again as she looked at Tad.

"That's a great promise," said the parson. "I'm glad you are rejoicing in that promise from God."

Tad wasn't sure what to say, so he thanked Laura for fixing his shirt. As he turned to leave he said, "Maybe I will see you both Sunday. Well, it was nice to meet you parson ... and, oh ... at what time?"

"Ten o'clock," came their simultaneous response ... which caused all three of them to laugh.

Tad went out to the buckboard with his shirt under his arm. Just as he got Old Buster headed up the street he heard a loud "Hey!" He looked around already knowing that voice from the day before, and saw Patch Gaines walking his way. Tad decided to wave and smile at him, and kept Old Buster headed home.

BIG DECISION ...

Tad got back to the ranch and showed his mom and dad the excellent repair Laura made to his shirt. He then asked them about going to church the coming Sunday. His mom said they used to go years ago when they would ride into town, catch a ferry over the Missouri River to St. Joseph where the nearest church was. Then they had to wait for a ferry back, and ride the buckboard back to the ranch ... taking up over a half- day in the process. "Our ranch work got behind and we often had to work late into the evening hours to make up for it. Horses don't know there is such a thing as Sunday! But ... now that there is a church in Tanner, we need to consider working that into our schedule. God has blessed us so much on our ranch. He's given us good health ... plenty of food ... a good ranch hand in Monty ... *and a great son!*" Then she looked at Porter and said, "Let's plan to do that Sunday. We need to rededicate ourselves to the Lord." Porter didn't have to even stop and think before he agreed with his wife that they owed God so much more than they could ever repay him, and that they should go this coming Sunday and make it a weekly habit. They would take a look at how they could balance the workload at the ranch perhaps by doing a little more on Saturday and a little more on Monday if necessary.

Then Tad revealed his true reason for wanting to go to church ... Laura would be there. "Oh-h-h-h-h," said his mom. "Now I see! That's still a good reason to go!"

Sunday came and the Rawlings put on some dressier clothes, and all three of them rode to church. As they stepped inside the door, Porter and Lucy spotted a couple they knew quite well. They thought they would like to sit with them, but Tad saw Laura and there was an empty spot next to her. His parents understood ... they were young once too!

After the service, Tad and Laura talked while his parents talked with her aunt and uncle, and also visited with some other people they hadn't seen in a while. Tad asked Laura if she had ever been to a rodeo. "No, but I have always wanted to go to one. I love horses even though we don't own any."

"There is a rodeo a ways west of here this coming Saturday. Would you like to go?"

"I'd love to", replied Laura. "Our business is open on Saturdays, but perhaps Aunt Molly can handle it alone. I'll go ask her." Laura went and stood by her aunt until she was finished talking. Tad's mind and heart grew in hopeful anxiety. Laura got her "okay" to be off on Saturday.

RODEO TIME ...

It seemed like a long week for Tad, but while he did his job well, his mind was already on Saturday. And Saturday finally came. He arrived with the buckboard at Laura's, but pulled by a horse better suited for the distance than Old Buster ... and nicer looking. He chose Donner, for he wanted to impress Laura in any and every way he could.

They talked about a lot of things on the way to the rodeo in Buckhorn. Tad told Laura about the loss of his parents, and mentioned how they were actually both orphans, but that he chose to call his aunt and uncle "Mom" and "Dad". Laura thought a moment and then said, "You know ... I think I'll start calling my aunt and uncle Mom and Dad too. I feel it in my heart ... I might as well say it with my lips."

Then Tad decided he needed to tell Laura about his confrontation with Patch Gaines, to see what she had to say about it. As he related what Patch told him about Laura being "his girl", and that Tad should stay away from her, Laura began to fume inside. She was very angry ... but even when angry she looked beautiful to Tad! She told Tad that Patch had confronted another guy who had come into her shop a couple of times. It scared the guy so much that he never came back to pick up his jeans that Laura had repaired. Molly had to go to the place where he lived to deliver them and that's when she found out the story. Tad thanked Laura for telling him the truth, and that he wouldn't worry about Patch any more. But Laura said, "Oh ... you do need to worry about him. He is unstable, and I have heard about threats he has made to others about being willing to 'gun anybody down' that comes near me." That left Tad with a lot to think about in how to handle Patch in the future, for he knew that nothing could keep him away from wanting to continue to date Laura. He had heard about "love at first sight" ... but now he had experienced it!

Tad and Laura got good seats at the outdoor rodeo ... and Laura seemed to be as involved with the excitement of the bronco busting and calf-roping as he was. The special skills and daring of these cowboys was fascinating to watch. What really caught Tad's eye was a trick rider who displayed amazing trick ways of riding a horse -- even two at the same time, standing up with a foot on each horse's back as they raced side-by-side and the cowboy holding the reins of both. Tad knew he would never try that, but then he watched as the cowboy approached his horse from the rear in a run, leaped up, put two hands on the horse's hind-quarters and vaulted forward into the saddle and took off! "Man," Tad said out loud. "I've got to master that myself!" Laura looked at him with her eyes wide open, astonished, and said, "You're not serious ... are you?"

"Yes. I'm serious," Tad said in a low tone of voice. "With practice, Blitzen and I can do that. Wait and see. I WILL do that." Laura was quiet. Running through her mind was the thought: 'What kind of a man's man cowboy am I sitting with?' Tad was thinking. He had a definite goal to achieve ... with Blitzen.

The ride back to Tanner found Laura and Tad getting even better acquainted. Tad pulled back on the reins on Donner when they got to her house. He walked her up to the door and they parted knowing they would see one another in church ... and both of them (secretly) couldn't wait!

WHEN TAD GOT HOME, he talked with his dad about how to handle the problem with Patch Gaines. He didn't want a confrontation, but didn't see how he could avoid it eventually. His dad said, "The best defense in this case is a good offense. There is a law that no firearms are allowed to be carried in town, so you don't have to worry about Patch having a gun. Your ranch work and work with the horses has you in very good physical condition. Patch Gaines is almost exactly your size, but probably much 'softer'. I would suggest that the next time he hollers 'Hey' to you and starts walking your way, that you walk directly toward him but at a slightly quicker pace than he is walking toward you. This will surely surprise him. When you meet, *be ready for anything.* He may try to sucker punch you in the stomach ... have your stomach muscles braced. He may swing for your head ... be ready to duck, and come up with an uppercut. If he decides to just talk, talk ... but don't let your mental guard down. Any more questions?"

"Uh-h-h. No!" Tad was quite surprised at his dad's advice ... but knew it was a winning approach. How he felt about Laura made anything necessary worthwhile.

On Monday, Tad began some personal training with Blitzen. He knew nothing about training a horse, but his dad gave him a few good ideas. He thought it would be a good idea for his horse to 'stay' when told to, and 'come' to him when told to. So he started by putting a lariat around Blitzen's neck, telling him to "Stay, Blitzen" ... and gradually walking away from him while holding the end of the lariat. When Blitzen started to follow him he again said, loudly, "Stay." Eventually Tad was able to get the full length of the lariat away ... at which time he then said "Come, Blitzen" ... and pulled on the lariat to encourage Blitzen to come toward him.

Much repetition seemed to do the trick for that day. But the next day it was like starting all over again ... so he did. Each day, a little more progress was made and it seemed as though both horse and 'trainer' were liking it.

SHOWDOWN ...

About mid-week Tad was looking for an excuse to see Laura again, so he asked his mom if she had anything that needed to go to Molly's Sewing and Repair Shop. She didn't, so Tad looked through his clothes ... found an old pair of jeans he didn't wear any more that had a hole in the knee. Good enough excuse to go to the shop!

As Tad rode the buckboard behind Old Buster into town, he wasn't far from the sewing shop when he heard the now familiar "Hey," from Patch Gaines. Tad halted Old Buster, saw Patch walking toward him, so he dismounted the buckboard, and, as his dad advised, walked toward Patch at a slightly faster gait than Patch was walking toward him. He saw an ever so slight surprise on Patch's face. As they met about an arm's length apart, Tad took the offensive saying in a firm voice while making unwavering eye contact, "Laura is **not** your girl, Patch. She told me so." Patch appeared to be speechless, but with a rising anger. Tad was braced for whatever Patch did. A few people had stopped walking on the boarded walk to watch this encounter which they knew was bound to happen sooner or later. Though Tad looked intently into Patch's eyes, he was conscious of Patch clenching his right fist, then quickly bringing it up and around in a right-hook fashion toward Tad's head. Tad quickly ducked, and then came up with a smashing uppercut that caught Patch squarely on his lower jaw and sent him reeling backwards, falling spread-eagle on his back in the street. He just lay there. Patch's fist had clipped the top of Tad's Stetson when he swung, knocking it to the dirt street. Tad picked up his hat, brushed some dirt off it, and said to Patch, "You got my hat dirty, Patch. Don't ever do that again. I like this hat!"

One of the men who had stopped to watch said, "You did the right thing, Tad. He's had that coming for a long time." An 'old timer' on the other side of the street chimed in, "Yer durn tootin'".

Tad got back on the buckboard, and went a few more yards to the sewing shop. He looked back, and Patch was just now slowly getting up ... and holding his jaw. Tad went inside with his old jeans to be repaired, and as he walked in the door Laura's and Molly's eyes were wide open, and Laura exclaimed, "WOW! Someone opened the door and told us to quick look out the window. WOW! Are you okay?"

"Sure," Tad said. "My fist hurts a little, but more important is how can this dirty spot on my hat be cleaned?"

"No problem," said Laura. She went in the back room and returned with the dirty spot completely gone. "No charge!"

"Gee," said Tad as he looked over his hat. "That's perfect! Thank you."

While Laura was in the back room, Tad had picked up a very small red feather that was on the floor. "What's this?" he asked Laura.

"Oh ... that was from a pretty decoration I made for a lady. She's already gone and that little feather won't be missed. You can have it. Put it in your hat band."

Tad slipped it in the front of his Stetson's hat band. "Hey ... that touch of color really looks great. Thanks." He showed Laura the hole in his old jeans. She told him the only thing she could do would be to take a large piece of denim material and sew it over the hole, but with the jeans being so faded compared to the new patch, it would look funny. So Tad decided to forget it. (It was only a ploy to have a reason to see Laura, anyway!) Tad said he would look forward to seeing her in church Sunday, and would she like to eat dinner afterwards at 'The Lucky Rose's Cafe' here in town. The answer was 'yes'.

THE MOST IMPORTANT DECISION ...

In church, Laura could tell that Tad had been listening intently to what Pastor Millard was saying, but this Sunday even more-so. After church they walked the few doors down to The Lucky Rose's Cafe', leaving the buckboard and Donner at the church. Tad's parents had come in a wagon hitched to Old Buster.

Tad had been quieter than usual since they left the church. They were seated at a table, and nodded and smiled at some other people from church who were already there. One of the owners of this family restaurant, Star, came over to take their orders. Laura introduced Star to Tad ... Laura and Star having been friends for some time.

After they ordered, Laura asked Tad what was on his mind. He said that he was trying to understand what Pastor Millard had meant when he said that a person had to make a *decision* to become a Christian. Laura replied, "Well, it's like a lot of other things in life that a person has to make a decision about -- what shoes or boots to put on today; where to live; what to do for a living. All of these have varying degrees of importance, but the decision of what to do about your relationship to God through Jesus Christ, is *the most important decision* one will ever make in life because it determines whether you will spend eternity in an unbelievably wonderful heaven with God ... or not!" Laura continued, "Jesus didn't just suffer excruciating pain and die on that cross because 'he got caught'. He was tried by a 'kangaroo court', and was condemned to death. But, what *really happened* was that God broke into history over eighteen-hundred years ago when he sent his Son to this earth for the express purpose of paying for your sins and mine -- and the whole world's -- by the shedding of his blood, and voluntarily giving His life. They didn't *take* His life ... He *gave* it! Eternal life is a free gift, but like any gift we have to accept it ... or reject it. The choice is one that each one of us has to make. *That's* the decision. If we accept this free gift of eternal life God has offered us through His Son ... we have forgiveness of all our sins, and *know* we have eternal life. I guess I could paraphrase John 3:16 as: *'For God so loved* **Tad Rawlings** *that He gave His only begotten Son, that if* **Tad** *believes in Him he will not perish but have everlasting life'.*"

"That's kinda' what I understood Pastor Millard to say," said Tad, " ... but hearing you explain it again makes it a little clearer now. That settles it ... I BELIEVE!" And with that, Tad, oblivious to the fact he was in a public restaurant, slammed his fist down on the table hard enough to make the silverware jump up!

It startled Laura so much she said, "Okay ... Okay." And as she embarrassingly looked around she saw everybody smiling. Some of the church members at other tables must have been aware of what was going on as they gave a 'thumbs up' sign as they smiled.

After the meal, Tad and Laura walked back to the church where Donner was waiting. On the way, Laura mentioned to Tad that Mr. Alexander Majors, who belongs to their church, had put a few signs up around town looking for young men to sign up for the Pony Express. One notice was posted next to their sewing shop door. She hadn't read it as Molly told him he could post it.

Donner pulled Tad and Laura to her house, and with no one around he gave her their first kiss. She went in the house and sat down ... a little dazed ... and thanked God for blessing her by bringing Tad into her life. Tad walked back to the buckboard ... his feet not touching the ground! He decided to ride over to Molly's shop and read what this Pony Express was all about. He got off the buckboard and went up to look at the notice pinned to the rough-boarded front of the shop. The notice read:

WANTED -- RIDERS FOR THE "PONY EXPRESS"
Riders to work in relay carrying the mail from here to Sacramento, California. <u>Requirements</u>: Young, skinny, wiry fellows not over 18. Must be expert riders willing to risk death daily. Orphans preferred. If interested, come to the new Pony Express office here in Tanner to be interviewed by Mr. Alexander Majors. Open noon to 5:00pm, Monday - Wednesday.

Reading this notice caused a rush of excitement in Tad Rawlings' mind. What an adventure! He determined to be at the Pony Express office tomorrow. He stepped out in the street and scanned the storefronts looking for a Pony Express sign. He spotted it. Now he needed to get back home and tell his dad about it.

Porter Rawlings told Tad he had heard about this new Pony Express, and that since it would take a large number of horses it could well be that Rawlings Ranch would be approached as a source of horses. He figured that Alexander Majors would be contacting him soon.

Well, Tad had some time to kill before suppertime, so he decided to build a "reasonable facsimile" of the rear of a horse up to and including the saddle. He had all the next morning to do his share of the chores around the ranch. He knew he couldn't practice this running vault on Blitzen that he had witnessed at the rodeo, until he had it nearly perfected on a dummy first. Blitzen would only take so much of a beating before just deciding to run off! One of their older barns had some spare lumber with which he made a support approximately horse-high with the top extra wide to support a saddle. He fastened a couple of angled side supports just forward of the saddle. Then he constructed a flat board at the rear, on which he would be planting his hands to make the vault up and forward into the saddle.

All finished, he thought he may as well give it a try. He took a couple of runs toward this horse mock-up without actually trying to vault up ... and he realized that the vaulting board needed to be raised to more accurately represent the height of Blitzen, so he modified it. He brought Blitzen over just so he could observe Tad and what he was doing. Then it was time to try it for real.

Ranch work had given Tad pretty strong upper-arms and shoulders, and that seemed to be the key to the success of his launch up and forward into the saddle. He ran through his memory, the picture of the cowboy at the rodeo, and what his form was as he did it so successfully. He got back about thirty feet and ran toward the "horse" ... but chickened out just before the launch and skidded to a stop. He went back again, took a deep breath, and began his run. He vaulted up and forward successfully, but landed on the rear part of the saddle ... and that didn't feel so good! Still, not bad for a first try. He felt the answer was to be running faster when he started the vault ... so the second time he was going at top speed when his two hands slammed down on the launching board and catapulted him up and forward ... right into the saddle.

He sat there a moment and shouted, "Whoopee ... I'm ready for the rodeo ... BIG time!"

Blitzen had been watching what Tad was doing, but of course he had no idea that he was also looking at "Blitzen, Junior" underneath that saddle. ... and that HE was next!

Tad thought he'd get his dad out to watch what he was doing and see if he had any suggestions. So Porter came out to observe. He mentioned to Tad that when his hands came down unexpectedly on the hind quarters of Blitzen it would surprise him and he might jerk one way or another, messing up everything. Tad thought back and he seemed to remember that the rodeo cowboy called out something to the horse before he did this routine. That got his horse accustomed to what was about to happen and not be surprised. Porter decided to sit on the corral fence and watch this son of whom he was so proud. Tad practiced some more, calling out "Ai-e-e-e-e Blitzen" when he started his run. And probably three-out-of-four vaults were just right. The mock-up horse was beginning to get a little wobbly, so Tad reasoned it was time to get Blitzen used to this action.

He started out by saddling Blitzen, and then, standing to one side in case Blitzen might kick backwards when hit on the hind quarters, he called out "Aie-e-e-e Blitzen", and a couple of seconds later slammed his hands on Blitzen's rear. Blitzen jumped a little the first few times, but seemed to get used to it ... and Tad followed the rear end 'whomp' with one on the saddle right afterwards. Tad decided to wait until the next day to do this same exercise with Blitzen again, and then the real thing if everything seemed to be going okay.

INTERVIEW ...

TAD HEADED TO THE PONY EXPRESS office about 1:00pm the next day. He sensed that Old Buster enjoyed getting out on these trips to town. He pulled a buckboard rather easily ... partly due to the regular greasing of the wheel hubs. All the Rawlings Ranch 'rolling stock' was kept in tip-top shape. As Tad started down the main street, he thought he saw Patch Gaines exiting the Pony Express office headed in the opposite direction. Tad tied Old Buster to a hitching post and went inside. There were a couple of other young guys, Jim and Graham, waiting to talk with Mr. Majors. He sat down and engaged them in speculative talk about this new Pony Express. They, like Tad, were pretty excited about it. They also mentioned that Patch Gaines left the office very mad. After Mr. Majors individually talked with Jim and Graham (and each one seemed happy after their respective interviews), Tad was called in.

Mr. Majors smiled and reached out to shake Tad's hand. They had met at church in the past. He told Tad that the Rawlings name was so respected in this part of Kansas, that if Tad was serious about signing on as a Pony Express rider, he had a special offer to make him ... and that was to be the *first rider* to leave the station at ten o'clock on Thursday morning, April 3rd, 1860. He went on to explain that it was so important for this new venture to get off to a good start. There would probably be a good size crowd on hand that morning, and he wanted a rider and a horse that looked every bit the part of a top-notch operation. He went on to say that the mail comes from Washington, DC and New York on a train to St. Joseph, Missouri, getting there about eight o'clock in the morning. Mr. Majors continued, "I'm employing one man to pick it up there, bring it over on the Missouri River Ferry to this office, getting here a little after nine. Some people are looking at it that the Pony Express begins in St. Joseph ... but I am looking at it like it starts from here. It's just a few blocks from the train to the Missouri River Ferry. That wouldn't be much of a send-off for a nineteen-hundred mile non-stop overland trip by horseback! Gotta get started here.

"Tad, we are making every effort to keep the weight down that these horses must carry. Special light-weight saddles will be used on every horse. Each horse will be traveling in the neighborhood of ten to fifteen miles to reach the next relay station -- which we have also called swing stations, or relief stations -- as quickly as possible without abusing the horses. There, the rider will get a fresh mount, and the mochila, which holds the mail, will be thrown over the saddle of the next horse ... and you're on your way again. About every seventy-five or eighty miles the relay station will be what I am calling a "home station". That is, a new rider will take over and keep heading west. The mail will never stop. There will be food and a bunk for you to be able to eat and rest up until the next series of rides you will be taking. I am hiring men only of a high caliber to manage each station. I am hiring riders only of a high caliber. I am buying horses only of a high caliber ... and I will want to talk with your dad as soon as I can. Perhaps tomorrow morning I will ride out to your place to talk with him. It is now March 1st, and we have just over a month to put everything together by our start date.

"As the first rider, Tad, I'm giving you a second choice that other guys won't be given: 1.) to sign on to ride, in relay, the entire distance to Sacramento, or 2.) to ride to the end of my jurisdiction which is six-hundred miles, plus or minus a few, and then make it a round-trip back here as a Pony Express rider just like when you were heading west ... except now you are heading east again. You may have some layover at that last home station before the mochila arrives from Sacramento ... and then again, it might be there just before you get there. At any rate, you are due your meal and rest. In fact there may be a layover in other home stations also, as it will depend on how often the mail comes here from the east. I do have to know what you want to sign on for, so I can plan the schedule and not have any gaps. We may have extra guys ... but no gaps! From the talk I've heard, many young men are looking forward to going to California ... may never get the chance again! The great majority of these young men will not have strong ties to this area like you do in family ... or girlfriend.

"Now ... about being the first rider. Oh ... pardon me ... I should ask if you have any questions before I go on."

"No. Sounds great so far ... so go on," replied Tad.

"The people who are here for the send off of the first rider will get their impression of the Pony Express by what they see that morning ... and that is what will be talked about. It can contribute greatly to the success and profitability of our goal to get the mail from here to Sacramento in ten days ... riding day and night and in all kinds of weather. Tad, don't put on any more weight, and if possible, drop ten pounds! My guess is you are over eighteen ... don't get any older!" They both got a good laugh over that. "But, Tad ... I have liked your appearance every time I have seen you. I'd like you to look on April 3rd, just like you look now … a Stetson better looking than mine! … neat and clean plaid shirt; good Lee trademark label on the back of your dungarees, and boots that shine. You will carry only four things with you: a water sack, a special edition of the Bible which I will give you; a horn to let the relay station know ahead of time to get the next mount ready; and a sidearm -- not a rifle as they are too heavy. But this can be a dangerous assignment at many places along the route. Dishonest men may try to stop you to take whatever might be in the mail you are carrying. Paiute Indians -- they are riled up as they don't want the white man taking any more of their land. But I don't know how far east they will be coming. Do you have a revolver and holster with a bullet belt? Can you shoot?"

Tad answered, "I don't have a gun now, but my dad has several. I can borrow one of his and do some practicing at the ranch."

"Pay will be one-hundred dollars a month, which is about three times what a person can earn around here in that time. Now, before we talk any more, I want to show you the oath that all riders are required to sign, and if you agree … sign it."

Tad read the oath:

"I, _____, do hereby swear, before the Great and Living God, that during my engagement, and while I am an employee of Russell, Majors, and Waddell, I will, under no circumstances, use profane language, that I will drink no intoxicating liquors, that I will not quarrel or fight with any other employee of the firm, and that in every respect I will conduct myself honestly, be faithful to my duties, and so

direct all my acts as to win the confidence of my
employers, so help me God."

Tad said, "I'll be glad to sign this, and because I have family
and a girlfriend here, I'll take the round trip back rides after the six-
hundred miles ... if I can hire on for six months."

"You got plans after six months?"

"I-I-I might have. I-I-I don't know yet." stammered Tad ...
thinking of Laura ... and their future.

"No problem," responded Mr. Majors. "You can always extend it
if you want to. I've heard the outside door open three or four more
times just since you've been in here. I don't think finding good young
men is going to be a problem. However, I do know I've made one
enemy already in Patch Gaines. He left here pretty mad. I didn't even
bother to interview him. He has a bad reputation, and well-earned.
I need also to tell you this ... since you are the first rider: you are to
keep the fact you are the first rider a secret from everyone except
your parents ... and they must be sworn to secrecy. Can you agree?"

"That sounds reasonable," said Tad. "But I have been dating
Laura Prescott from church, and need to let her know I will be gone
a while. She can be trusted completely ... and, she probably needs to
feel free to tell her parents"

"No problem on that young man. I've known her, and her aunt
and uncle for many years. Good Christian people. Just be sure they
know it goes no further."

Then Tad said: "One more thing. I would like to ride Blitzen for
this first leg ... to the first relay station. He will give you the best start
of any horse you could pick. However ... he's my horse and we can't
sell him to you. But, I can loan him for this ride."

"Huh! I hadn't planned on that ... but I don't see as that would be a problem. Plus you'll save me a couple of hundred bucks or more!"

Tad leaned over and was excited to sign his name on the oath document.

Mr. Majors handed Tad a map of the first third of the Pony Express route -- about six-hundred miles -- showing where all the relay and home stations were located. At that last home station, he would then pick up the mochila that is going from west-to-east when it arrives. Most stations of both types were in small towns, but where towns were few and far between, new stations (not much more than a shack and a small stable) were being built. "Tell your dad I'll be out to his ranch tomorrow morning. Gotta' get back here by noon for more interviews."

LOOKING OVER THE STOCK ...

AND SURE ENOUGH about ten o'clock the next morning Alexander came to the ranch to talk with Porter. These two men knew one another from church, and just over the years as good citizens of Tanner. They had great respect for each other. Alexander started off by telling Porter that he and two partners, William H. Russell and William B. Waddell, were each responsible for one-third of the approximate nineteen hundred miles to Sacramento. He didn't need just 'horses' ... but *good* horses. He knew the Rawlings' Ranch had the best in the business. Good horses cost good money, and he was prepared to pay it.

Porter walked him out to see the horses that were relatively nearby on the ranch. Alexander looked at them up close and said, "I know horse-flesh, and these are the healthiest horses I have ever seen. I understand where you got your reputation. What do you do differently than other ranchers?"

"I guess if I have to have a little secret from you (thinking about the wade-berry over in a small pasture he was not exposing to any visitor who came to his ranch) ... that will have to be it." Porter smiled at his friend ... and as a businessman himself, Alexander understood ... and smiled back.

Porter reasoned if he sold off all but a small number of his choice horses it would be an amazing amount of money, and he could take his time in breeding more excellent horses for the future. It would cut way back on the amount of work needed on the ranch, so with Tad following through on being a Pony Express rider, he and Monty could handle the work load with time to spare.

Alexander easily agreed on Porter's price-per-horse, and said he would take all that he would sell. Porter told him how many that was and they shook hands. That is all anyone who made a deal with this ranch owner needed ... just a handshake. Porter had said to many people, *"If a man can't trust your handshake, he can't trust your signature"*. He lived and ran his business that way. Everyone in Tanner ... and even the mid-west ... knew it. There was no man held in greater respect for his character and integrity than Porter Rawlings. And certainly Alexander Majors would be in that same category.

TAD HAD WORKED with Blitzen a little more on the 'come' and 'stay' commands, and that training appears to be complete. All that is needed is to go through it on occasions so he doesn't forget. Now the big test: getting the rear mount perfected.

Tad got his dad to finish the work he was doing so he could watch him work with Blitzen, and offer any suggestions. He ran through the 'whomp' on the hind quarters followed by one on the saddle, and preceded by "Aie-e-e-e Blitzen," many times. Blitzen was now getting used to it. At first he was turning his head around, but now didn't even do that. Porter mentioned to him that the call to Blitzen from a distance instead of right next to him, plus the sound of running footsteps would be new to the horse's ears. Tad hadn't thought of that, so he practiced getting back about thirty feet, making the call, running up behind Blitzen and doing the two 'whomps'. Blitzen noticed a little difference, but after three or four of these dry runs, it was now time to do the real thing.

Tad walked back behind Blitzen, looked over at his dad, who nodded, and let out a loud "Aie-e-e-e Blitzen" and sprinted forward. His hands landed perfectly, and he landed in the saddle ... slightly to one side, but in the saddle. His dad let out with applause, and came over with a smile on his face to shake hands with his son for this accomplishment. Tad repeated this several more times, and followed that with a "Giddyap". It then got to where Blitzen didn't even need to hear the "Giddyap" ... just took off as soon as Tad hit the saddle. Tad felt really good about the training of this horse. He thought he just might use this mount to dazzle the crowd at the start of the Pony Express! ... and not even tell Mr. Majors so he could be surprised.

AN UNUSUAL FIREARM ...

NOW ... THE OTHER THING he needed to work on was getting his dad to loan him a revolver with gun belt. As Tad had grown older, Porter and Lucy had more and more confidence in their son ... especially since he came into a really close walk with the Lord. So when he told his dad that Mr. Majors said he needed to carry a revolver on his rides Porter immediately took him to a small collection of rifles and handguns, all of which Tad had seen before. But this time Porter brought out one that he had hidden away for safe keeping. It stunned Tad when he saw it. It was a Colt 45, holstered with a band of bullets all around the waist. What a beauty! And the remarkable thing was that the barrel of the six-shooter extended over two inches below the bottom of the holster! Porter said, "If you've got to carry a side-arm for protection, this is the weapon to carry." He held it out to Tad who cradled it in both hands with awe.

"It's a beauty, Dad. What's the deal with such a long barrel on a pistol?"

"Good question," replied his dad. "Most people think that the barrel of a gun, whether a pistol or a rifle, is just a straight hole down the center in which the bullet travels. Actually, there are shallow grooves that curve down the barrel in order to impart a spin to the bullet as it is accelerating forward from the powerful explosion that just occurred behind it. Without that, what we call "rifling" within the barrel, the bullet would tend to wobble a lot in flight as the air reacts to the projectile piercing through it. This added wind resistance would slow the bullet down and it would not travel as far. The extra long barrel on this particular Colt 45 means the bullet will have that spinning force exerted on it for a longer time and stabilize the bullet even more, thereby making this revolver more accurate at a longer range than one with a short barrel."

"You sure know a lot, Dad."

His dad laughed, putting his arm around Tad's shoulders, "Ha, ha, ha … you know a whole lot more than I did at your age."

Porter took Tad out to the side of the ranch house away from the horses. He grabbed a couple of tin cans from the trash on the way out and set them on a tree stump that was about thirty-five feet away. Porter put six bullets in the revolver, took aim and fired twice. He hit one of the tin cans. Porter went over and put it back up on the stump, then handed the revolver to Tad saying, "These bullets are fairly old … there may be some that won't fire. Now, you don't just 'pull' the trigger. You squeeze the entire hand to equalize the force on the gun so it doesn't pull off target by just getting force upon it from one direction. Plus, it stabilizes the pistol more when the gun powder explodes. Tad took aim and pulled the trigger four times … the third time was a misfire. He hit one can. His dad said, I have some fresh bullets in the house, but lets use up all these in the gun belt first to get rid of any bad ones. Tad used them up, resetting the tin cans several times … and three more bad cartridges were found. His aim improved to where he hit a can each time. His dad told him to use the box of cartridges in the house for target practice, and just plain getting used to this firearm. And … to be sure to pick up another box when in town, so he can load the gun belt with fresh bullets when he hit the Pony Express trail.

"Your mom has been a little quieter lately, after hearing you wanted to be a Pony Express rider. But she's coming around. She knows you are an adult now, and wants you to do what you feel is God's will for your life. And if that is the Pony Express, she is fine with it. But, naturally, she will worry. I will too, but probably not as much!"

TAD KNEW THAT LAURA was going to be off work on Thursday, and they had planned on taking a buckboard ride to an oasis-like area a few miles southwest of Tanner. Laura's "mother" (now) packed them both a lunch. To sum up the experience that day, would be to say that they both continued to get to know one another better 'n better. Both came from a solid, Christian-based home life. Both were very grateful for the way God had kept them alive, in spite of the terrible accidents both of their parents had suffered. Though unspoken as yet, it seemed to each of them that God had prepared them for each other … for this life. When Tad mentioned to Laura about his job being the first Pony Express rider, and that she needed to keep that an absolute secret, she was speechless … as she knew that would mean he would not be around here for longer than she cared to think about. He explained that the money he would earn, and not having any expenses, would all be saved for whatever the future held. She got kinda' quiet. Tad let her know that his future included seeing her as much as possible. … and that they both could do a lot of thinking about that.

AFTER CHURCH ONE SUNDAY, Alexander Majors pulled Tad aside, and let him know that the first ride may well be the most dangerous. Potential bandits would know the exact start of this ride -- ten o'clock on April 3rd -- because it is being so well publicized all over in an effort to build up the mail business and therefore make it profitable. The time when a Pony Express rider may pass any given point farther along the route would be totally unknown ... but they would know he was leaving Tanner at ten, headed west. "Have you got a good shootin' iron yet?" Alexander asked.

"The best," answered Tad.

"Are you feeling afraid?"

"Not a bit! Dad loaned me his long-barreled Colt 45, plus, Blitzen and other Rawlings' horses can outrun any horse in Kansas and points west if needed."

"You give me a lot of confidence that we are off to a good start, Tad. Thanks, and may God bless you. Just a few more days ..."

WHEN TAD WASN'T HELPING his dad and Monty with the usual work required to raise quality horses, he was doing target practice. He got to where he could hit those cans every time at a longer distance than he practiced with his dad. Even shooting from the hip he had good accuracy. For the fun of it, he tried the same shooting, but with a Colt 45 that had a standard length barrel ... and he saw the difference; he needed to be much closer to hit the target.

Other time was spent riding Blitzen around their large ranch for an extended period of time at a little faster than a trot ... maybe a "slow gallop" ... what he figured would be a good speed for fifteen miles or so on the Pony Express route. Sometimes he urged Blitzen into a full gallop ... what would be termed 'interval' training. Much would depend on the topography of the trail. Tad "whooped it up" as he was riding Blitzen to get some of the other horses that Alexander Majors would be putting into Pony Express duty, into following along. Many did. This built up their stamina more even though most of the horses loved running from time-to-time around the large fenced-in ranch acreage. Some of the horses that did not follow Blitzen's lead,

Tad saddled up and road them the same way ... getting more to follow suit. One day Alexander Majors came by with some men and took possession of the Rawlings Ranch horses he had purchased. He and his team had to distribute them to the immediate relay stations, and then he had to pick up more horses he had bought farther along the route ... and distribute them.

PORTER AND LUCY thought it might be nice to invite Laura and her parents over for dinner after church the Sunday before Tad would be 'galloping off into the sunset'. About mid-week, since the coming Sunday would be the last before the Pony Express started, Tad hooked up Old Buster and went into Tanner to have a little chat with Mr. Majors, and check with Laura and her mom in their shop about dinner the coming Sunday. Just as he was dismounting the buckboard, Mumps and BB spotted him and hollered, "Hey, Dude. Sure Old Buster ain't too fast fer ya'?" Tad smiled and waved to them ... which always shut them up. All went well in his meeting with Mr. Majors, and Laura's mom was grateful for the invitation. So, on Sunday, the six of them -- the Rawlings and the Prescotts -- had a great time around the dinner table ... then relaxing in the large western-style den most of the afternoon.

"RIDE, COWBOY, RIDE ..."

THE 10 A.M. SENDOFF for the beginning of the Pony Express was drawing near. Townspeople, farmers, ranchers, and even people from towns around -- some from St. Joseph across the river -- were beginning to line the street on both sides from the Pony Express office and heading westward out of town. The mail from the east coast had arrived in St. Joseph and ferried across the Missouri River, and was now being inserted and locked into the compartments of the mochila. Alexander Majors had arranged for a dozen or so men to work on keeping the crowd back along the sides of the street. Everybody cooperated, and it allowed everyone to see better. It was pretty exciting for these folks to witness such an important part of history unfolding before their eyes ... the connection of mail service between the east coast and the west coast, by a series of dedicated riders who knew there was unexpected danger. There were bandits, rain and lightening at any point along the route ... and danger from Paiute Indians.

Since it was partly Alexander Majors' money that was invested in the horses, station masters, buildings at the relay stations and home stations along the nineteen hundred miles to Sacramento, California, he could call the shots ... and he had insisted that the first rider's name be kept secret. He didn't want the first rider to be pestered with questions for days leading up to the start -- or be a target for those angered because he had not picked them for this sought-after job.

At five minutes before ten o'clock, Zippy, the station master, brought Blitzen out from behind the station and into the street.

People were awed at the beauty of this magnificent steed that stood before them facing west. Shiny dark-brown coat, muscle definition of shoulders and hind quarters ... ready to be mounted for the first leg of the journey. What a horse! Ranchers who knew horses well, knew this was a Rawlings horse not only from its healthy appearance, but also from the white cross-cornered stockings on its right front and left rear legs.

Then Tad Rawlings, side by side with Mr. Majors, strode out of the Pony Express station office. They stopped at the edge of the boarded walk, and Alexander gave a short speech -- not more than a minute in length -- of gratitude for the support of all who were present for this historic moment in history. He introduced Tad Rawlings as the first rider, and led in a short prayer for Tad's safety and the safety of all the riders that will come after him. There was some applause at the end of the prayer, as the name Rawlings was endeared to this town. As usual, Tad was wearing the best looking Stetson around. Unusual, was the long-barreled Colt 45 holstered with extra bullets strapped around his hips. It was the first time any person had worn a firearm in town since the law against it was passed fifteen years before. Tad parted the crowd and walked to the middle of the street where Zippy was holding the reins of Blitzen. He then flung the "mochila" mail pouch across the saddle, with its four locked cantinas (compartments) -- two on each side. The rider actually sat on the leather mochila during the ride, with a cantina in front of and behind both knees. At each stop the rider simply lifted it off and put it over the saddle on the next mount ... and he was on his way again. Mumps and BB arrived belatedly, and stood at the edge of the crowd. BB hollered out, "Hey Dude. You're not going to try to ride that horse are you? You'd better stick to Old Buster." The two of them with rolled cigarettes dangling from the corners of their respective mouths, then laughed and slapped each other on the back. Tad smiled.

After looking over the saddle cinching, patting Blitzen on the shoulder and running a gloved hand over his nose, he walked back a ways behind Blitzen. Tad turned around, took a deep breath, hollered "Aie-e-e-e Blitzen", and ran toward his horse. He leaped up and with his two hands landing on Blitzen's hind quarters, he vaulted forward right into the saddle and Blitzen took off in an accelerated sprint.

Zippy was so caught up in this totally unexpected start, as was the entire crowd, that he took off his hat, waved it in the air and hollered, "**Ride, cowboy, ride!**" This caught on with those on both sides of the street, and as Tad galloped past them they, too, waved their hats and called out, "Ride, cowboy, ride." The thunder and increasing tempo of Blitzen's hoof beats echoed down the main street and could be heard above the cries. Laura and Molly had brought two short stools out from their shop and stood on them on the boarded walk so they could see above the crowd. As Tad rode by with Blitzen at top speed by this time, he spotted Laura and took off his Stetson and waved. Laura mouthed the words, "Ride, *my* cowboy, ride." Porter and Lucy stayed on the buckboard behind Old Buster near the end of the street as that made them higher than those standing, and could easily see their son as he galloped past … again taking off his Stetson and waving to them. Tad and Blitzen left on the trail out of town, but he could still hear the fading cries of "Ride, cowboy, ride." "Ride, cowboy, ride." "Ride, cowboy, ride."

Mumps and BB were so caught off guard by this magnificent display of horsemanship that their mouths dropped open and both cigarettes landed in the dirt simultaneously.

Alexander Majors stood there watching as Tad disappeared from sight. Those around him heard him say in a low tone of voice, "I think an awful lot of that young man." One who overheard was Laura Prescott's father ... and he felt the same way.

ONE ANGRY HOMBRE' ...

What no one noticed was a deeply angry and hostile Patch Gaines who saw Tad Rawlings get the honor and glory that rightfully belonged to him. He went behind the General Store, got on his pinto horse and galloped behind the stores and out of town on a somewhat parallel road to the Pony Express route. The route to Sacramento was carefully laid out with the stamina of the horses in mind. There were areas where the Pony Express trail was more level than the absolute shortest path ... and not too far from Tanner was one of those areas. Unusual for the flatlands of Kansas was the Brainard Rock Quarry which the Pony Express route skirted in favor of a more level trail, although it was slightly longer.

Patch Gaines spurred his horse onward, and planned to take the quarry route and thereby get to the junction where the two trails merged before Tad did. Yes, it took a lot out of a horse in climbing the quarry steeps, and risking uncertain footing at anything faster than a trot, but Patch aimed to get to the overlook above the junction in time to train his rifle sight on the unsuspecting Pony Express rider below. Patch wasn't worried about the extra energy his pinto would use up in going this route as he wasn't going as far as Tad's horse had to travel.

There were some short stretches along the Pony Express route where you could see the quarry path ... maybe three-hundred yards away. It was in one of those spots that Tad happened to see Patch riding the only pinto horse he knew of in that part of the country ...

the dark brown and snow white pattern standing out plainly. Tad reasoned that danger lie ahead of him at the junction a couple of miles down the trail. If Patch shot him there, no witnesses would be around, and he would be rid of the guy who had won the heart of the girl he could not have … and who had stolen the notoriety he wanted for himself by being the first Pony Express rider.

Revenge … what a terrible path in life to take, but Patch was on that trail. There was fire in his eyes and hatred in his heart.

At another spot where Tad could see the quarry trail, he could see that Patch was a good bit ahead of him … and he did the only thing he could think of to avert the success of what he thought was Patch's plan, and that was to cut over to the quarry trail a good ways behind Patch. He spurred Blitzen diagonally "cross-country" to the quarry trail. The really rugged part of that route was past. This would make Tad late to arrive at the relay station to pick up a fresh mount, but if he fell into Patch's trap he wouldn't get there at all.

He slowed Blitzen's pace down a bit so he could always see a good bit ahead. When he was about a hundred yards from the junction overlook he dismounted from Blitzen, dropped the reins and told him to "stay". He was taking no chances of an approaching horse giving a warning to Patch … if indeed he was waiting at the overlook.

Tad moved quickly but quietly on foot toward the overlook, and as he drew close he unholstered his long-barrel Colt forty-five. He had no plans to use it unless absolutely necessary. He had a good job he was being paid to do and that was to successfully get the mail through multiple relay stations, and multiple changes of horses, to where the next rider would take over.

CONFRONTATION ...

Tad very carefully moved up the incline to the overlook. Over to one side he saw the pinto, so he knew Patch was there and watching the trail for Tad to arrive. He spotted Patch leaning against a large boulder with his rifle pointed toward the trail. Tad moved ever so quietly until he was less than thirty feet behind Patch. Tad had thought deeply about what his plan should be as he was riding cross-country to get on Patch's trail. Now the time had come to implement it.

With his feet set, and his revolver pointed right at Patch, he boomed out, "Drop that rifle, Patch, or you're a dead man." Patch nearly jumped out of his skin and his rifle clattered to the ground. A look of fear and terror was on his face as he spun and faced the long-barreled six-shooter pointed right at him.

"D-d-d-don't shoot," Patch was finally able to say.

Tad let about twenty seconds go by before speaking again. He wanted Patch to think about the entire situation that was transpiring. It seemed more like five minutes to Patch ... when you're looking down the barrel of a gun, and you can even see the tips of the bullets in the rotating revolver chamber of this powerful sidearm.

"Move over to your left a good ways away from that rifle, Patch."

Patch was clearly scared, but he managed to get a weak bluff out: "I'm not movin'. You're not about to pull that trigger." With his Colt 45 at hip level Tad pulled the trigger and a lead slug slammed into the boulder just six inches from Patch's right hip. Stone chips flew from the impact, some hitting Patch's hand. He recoiled from the sting, and now clearly scared, he moved a good ways from the rifle. Tad walked over and picked up the rifle without taking his eyes off Patch. He glanced at the rifle and saw Patch's name engraved on the stock.

"Now ... here's the plan Patch; you'd better listen up:

"I am taking your rifle with me, and due to its added weight, will hide it somewhere along the trail ... and pick it up whenever I get back this way. I will be giving it to Sheriff Johnson to keep until you can be trusted with it. Just in case anything happens to me, I will be relating exactly what you did today to the next two station masters. They will be sworn to secrecy unless something happens to me ... at which time they will get in touch with the sheriff.

"Patch, I know you have had a hard upbringing and I am real sorry about that. I lost both my parents in a boulder rockslide up in Dakota Territory when I was only four-years-old. But God allowed me to be brought up by my aunt and uncle here in Tanner. To me, they are just like my mom and dad. Through no fault of your own, you don't have a mother around, and your dad thinks more of his own life than he does of yours ... and hasn't given you the love and upbringing I have been so fortunate to have. However, you are an adult now and must take responsibility for your own decisions. You have not been doing well in that regard ... and that needs to change. Some weeks ago I became a Christian, and God changed me from the inside out. That's what you need ... but **you** have to make the decision. No one can do it for you.

"So ... I will be willing to forget what happened today on one condition: that you make an appointment with Pastor Millard at the church. Sit down with him and ask him the question, 'What do I need to do to become a Christian?' You listen to him closely, and come back on a later date to see how you are doing. If you allow Jesus Christ to change you like he changed me, you get your rifle back. If you don't, then I will be taking this rifle with your name on it to the sheriff and telling him the entire story."

"It will just be your word against mine," Patch replied. "I can tell him you stole the rifle from me."

"Because my dad and mom have such a good reputation with the sheriff and everybody else in this part of the country ... the word of a Rawlings is as good as gold against any other story. I'm a Rawlings. Who do you think the sheriff will believe?"

Patch just sort of dropped his gaze, and Tad could tell he looked very defeated.

"You've caused me to run behind on this very important job," Tad said, intentionally showing some anger, "so I've got some time to make up. Think about what I have said, Patch. Your future depends upon it." Tad looked Blitzen's way and hollered, "Blitzen ... come!" Immediately his horse responded by trotting right to where Tad was still holding a gun on Patch. With his gun in his right hand, rifle under his arm, and the reins in his left, Tad walked to where Patch's pinto was standing. He let go of Blitzen's reins and took hold of the pinto's. He then turned him back toward the quarry trail, walked him forward in the direction of Tanner a few yards, hollered "Get goin'," and slapped him hard on his hind quarters. The pinto took off ... and jinxed Patch's ability to go anywhere until he could catch up with his horse. Tad holstered his forty-five, tied the rifle behind the saddle and mounted Blitzen. He hollered "Good luck," to Patch, and spurred Blitzen forward to the junction just ahead where he got back on the designated Pony Express trail.

Tad couldn't see it, but Patch slumped to the ground. As he sat there, he picked up a rock and threw it. Totally defeated in life … Patch cried for the first time since he was a young boy.

BACK ON TRAIL ...

Blitzen had had some rest, so Tad felt okay about urging him into gallop mode to make up at least some of the time he lost. But he felt good ... and said a prayer for Patch.

Tad knew he needed to heed Alexander Major's warning about anything that looked suspicious along the route. In the open as he was riding now, he could relax. In areas where there were woods, curves in the trail, large boulders ... he needed to be keenly aware of anything. He slowed Blitzen down to a walk so he could empty out the shell casing from his forty-five ... the one he had just used on Patch ... and inserted another bullet. He wanted a six-shooter, not a five-shooter! Back up to nearly full speed on the open plains.

Another four miles and Tad saw the stream up ahead that he and Blitzen would have to ford. There were trees and shrubbery on both sides of the stream, so Tad was keenly aware of the chance of trouble in this situation. He slowed Blitzen down some so he could scan both sides of the trail up ahead. They forded the stream which was about two feet deep, and Tad observed both sides of the trail on the other bank as they approached. Coming out of the stream, using the utmost caution, he could see all around very well. This was a good place to leave Patch's rifle. He halted Blitzen, walked three trees in and propped it up on the far side of that tree. Back on Blitzen, and in thirty yards it was open plains again. This was typical Kansas country. The first relay station, where he and Blitzen would part company, was three miles ahead in a small town ... so Tad urged his mount on at a good speed, aware they had lost some time when he had to deal with Patch. Blitzen seemed strong and not at all tired from the journey. He was a good horse. No ... he was a *great* horse!

Galloping into Wardsville, Tad spotted the Pony Express sign and readied himself for a quick change of horses. He was afraid to use the horn that Mr. Majors had given him. He didn't want to blow something loudly from a hundred yards away ... something that could easily scare a horse when blown unexpectedly from just behind his ears. A man named Jensen was in charge of this station ... mostly feeding, watering and caring for the horses. Jensen was out in front of the station when Tad pulled up. Tad was expecting to see another Rawlings horse saddled, ready and waiting ... especially since he was later than expected. But Jensen had bad news.

"The horse for the next relay isn't doing too good," he told Tad. "I'm suspecting it is bad feed. He looks kinda' listless ... just not up to par for a horse from the Rawlings' stable. He seemed perfectly fine when he was brought here five days ago. I'm sure it's not the water cuz I got that myself from the spring. Drank some of it too, and I feel fine. I'm gonna' have to take the rest of the feed back to where I got it and get some from another source. You got a fine lookin' mount there. Never saw a horse with those cross-cornered stockings before. That's really something. Is he up to doing another thirteen miles? He sure looks great. And, by the way, that is one good lookin' cowboy hat ... finest I've ever seen." Talkative guy, this Jensen ... smiled as he talked. "What's the deal on that little red feather? Gotta' be a story behind that!" So Tad took off his Stetson and told him. He paused a moment and looked at the feather. ... and thought of Laura. When would he see her again? Jensen went on, "Wow! That's some kind of firearm yer packin' on yer hip. You are well equipped!"

Tad was quiet ... and sorry he hadn't held Blitzen back a little more on his pace the last stretch. He looked Blitzen over carefully ... his mouth ... felt his shoulders ... checked his feet and shoes. Other than a slight sweat he looked just like he did when he left Tanner. Tad said, "Well ... as they say, 'Ya gotta do what cha' gotta do.' And I guess that means Blitzen does another thirteen miles. He doesn't need any feed, thankfully," he told Jensen, "but he could sure use some water since you are sure it's okay."

"Stake my life on it," Jensen said with a big smile that showed a couple of teeth missing.

As Tad, Jensen and Blitzen walked to where the water was stored, he told Jensen about his confrontation with Patch, and swore him to secrecy unless he heard later that something happened to him. "In that case, go to the wooded area on this side of the last stream I crossed, get the rifle from behind a tree on the right side -- it's in about three trees from the trail -- take it to Sheriff Johnson in Tanner and relate what I have told you." Jensen agreed, and Tad knew he could trust him as he had been interviewed carefully for this responsible position. And Jensen had a warning for Tad: "Outside of town you've got a couple of miles of open country. Then the trail curves through a small area of some trees. There have been more holdups and ambushes in that area than anywhere else in this part of the country. Be careful."

Even as Tad had rode into Wardsville he was keeping his eyes open for anything suspicious. As he stopped at the Pony Express station, he had noticed two men get off a bench in front of the General store, get on their horses rather quickly and gallop out of town on the trail he would be using.

After Tad was sure that Blitzen had had enough water, he waved goodbye to Jensen and trotted Blitzen through town. Many people were looking at this unusual horse with the cross-cornered stockings; the nice looking rider; the mochila with the four cantinas. They waved and smiled at Tad, knowing they were witnessing the first day of the Pony Express.

THE SECOND 'LEG' -- BANDITS ...

The few minutes rest at that station had been good for Blitzen, but Tad was not as concerned about making up lost time now as he was for his horse. He kept Blitzen at sort of a loping gallop in the open country outside of town. Ordinarily he would have been riding a fresh horse a little faster, but he wanted to save Blitzen in case he really needed to call on his speed if they got in trouble. Tad slowed Blitzen to a trot as they approached the trees and shrubs and the curve in the trail that Jensen had warned him about. With squinted eyes Tad searched for anything unusual on both sides of the trail. If he put Blitzen in a full gallop to get through it quickly he might not spot serious trouble in time. Way back over to the right he spotted a couple of horses partially hidden by brush. One was solid black ... like one of the guys had ridden out of town.

Watching both sides of the trail, Tad's eyes picked up the sight of a rope tied around a tree trunk about eighteen inches above the ground and going straight across the trail to another tree. He knew Blitzen wouldn't see it, as the rope was the same color as the dirt trail. It was really only visible where it tied around the dark tree trunks on both sides. Tad quickly veered Blitzen to the left, off the trail, and around that tree. As Blitzen was stepping back on the trail, Tad heard, then saw, some movement in the bushes on the right. He pulled out his Colt 45 and fired into that brush. He immediately heard a yell of pain, and he put Blitzen into a gallop. Then he heard a gunshot, looked around and saw one guy standing in the middle of the trail firing a pistol at him. Tad and Blitzen were now out of accurate range for a typical forty-five, if that was what he was using, so Tad brought Blitzen to a sudden halt. With his arm out straight, he carefully pointed his long-barreled forty-five at the guy in the middle of the trail, raised the tip of the barrel some because of the distance, and squeezed the trigger just like he had done in target practice. The bushwhacker yelled, grabbed his hip and spun to the ground. Tad reholstered his firearm and again put Blitzen into a full gallop. He didn't want to take any chances that there might be other bandits around. But, they were quickly into the wide open spaces again. He looked around after covering a half-mile, saw no one, so he slowed Blitzen down, patted him on the side of the neck and said, "Good job, Blitzen." If horses could talk, Blitzen would surely have said, "Good job, Tad."

Tad felt bad about shooting those two bushwhackers ... and leaving them. But they are simply paying for their own sins ... the hard way. And, he is getting paid for the job of getting this mail through to the next rider. Anything, or anyone, that gets in the way has to be dealt with in the most effective way possible. A properly placed bullet is the only thing bandits understand. Tad slowed Blitzen to a walk as he emptied the two shell casings from his forty-five and again restored it to its six-bullet capacity. Three empty spots now appeared on his belt-of-bullets. Now it's back up to a faster pace since he was still a little behind.

THE NEXT RELAY STATION, in Fronter, was just up ahead. He knew Blitzen needed water, and extended rest. Fortunately there was another Rawlings horse ready to go when he got there. He left notice with the station keeper that Blitzen was his personal horse and was only to go back toward Tanner … not toward Sacramento. When it got to Tanner, Mr. Majors was to be notified, and the horse returned to the Rawlings Ranch. The station keeper understood and promised those directions would be followed. Tad also told him about the attempt on his life by Patch. He told him where the rifle was, and what to do if anything happened to him. … just like he told Jensen.

Tad took off at a good speed. The horse he was riding now had seemed like he recognized Tad when he saw him. Well, he should … he had been around him since birth!

Open country and a fresh Rawlings horse … life doesn't come much better than that for a Pony Express rider. Tad then got to the next swing-relay station and changed horses in less that a minute. Still open country and a good trail. More typical of Kansas than his early riding. Station after station, good horse after good horse … the Pony Express was off to a good start, in spite of some unexpected events! Another relay station came and went, and Tad is on another strong Rawlings horse. According to his map, the next station will be a "home station," which means he turns the mochila over to another rider. The home station is in a small town, and Tad will be able to relax until his next series of rides. He was looking forward to it, but didn't seem to be very tired. He mostly felt like he needed to do some deep-knee bends, twist his upper body, jog a little … kinda' loosen up some muscles and tendons that don't get much use while riding a horse.

Tad pulled into Payton Wells and spotted the Pony Express sign. The station was larger than the others as it had a room for bunks and another room for eating meals. It was the station keeper's responsibility to provide for the riders. An unsaddled horse was out front. Tad dismounted and took the mochila inside. Jim, the station keeper, told Tad he had some bad news -- the rider who was supposed to ride the next legs, had broken his the day before! Tad couldn't believe it. Jim told him he would be glad to be the rider and Tad be the station tender except for the fact his wife was expecting a baby at any time. "You've ridden eighty miles or more." Jim said. "I wouldn't blame you if you just quit."

Tad was quiet ... thinking over the options he and the Pony Express had. He finally decided: "Jim, you unsaddle the mount I came in on. Lead him to where he can get some food and water, and then saddle the fresh horse while I take an out-house break, do a few exercises, eat a sandwich or two, and drink whatever you have ... preferably good water. *The mail must go through.* That is what I signed on to do." Jim was excited at the dedication of this young cowboy. He ran out the door, unsaddled Tad's horse and led him around to the small barn in back where there was hay, feed and water. He saddled up the fresh horse -- another Rawlings -- while Tad did some jumping-jacks after taking off his weapon belt. Tad was oblivious to the stares he was getting ... and smiles ... from the townspeople. Tad simply smiled back. He was task oriented, had a good Christian work ethic, and his mind was on what lay ahead ... not on what an exercising cowboy looked like to strangers!

Tad put the mochila on the fresh mount, looked at his map and saw that after another half-dozen relay stations, that Bremming would be his next chance to sleep and eat. He said goodbye to Jim after spending about twenty minutes in Payton Wells ... eighteen longer than the schedule called for! Jim assured him that the trail ahead to the next home station in Bremming was a good trail and totally in open country except for a couple of small-town relay stations that provide a welcome change of scenery. Other relay stations had to be built because the distance between towns was farther than horses could travel at speed. However, it was now around six o'clock and dusk would be creeping in slowly as he crossed into Nebraska Territory -- the people there clamoring for statehood that was still seven years in the future. If there were no more interruptions in the flow of things, he figured he should get through all the relay stations and reach the next home station well after midnight ... perhaps one a.m. And things did go well. The starry skies and a waxing three-quarter-moon gave him excellent visibility right to his bunk in the home station in Bremming. One weary cowboy ... and a job well done.

INDIAN DANGER ...

TAD WAS GETTING TO SEE much of America, and getting paid
to do it! However, he was warned it was a dangerous job. The danger
was there, but he was trusting God to get him through it. The home
station had water buckets so he could take a reasonable facsimile of a
bath. Mr. Majors even thought so far ahead as to have an assortment
of clean underwear and socks for the riders.

Becoming a Pony Express rider was a tough decision; being away
from Laura and his mom and dad for so long. But he couldn't pass
up the opportunity to do something exciting ... and to help pave the
way for the "taming of the west."

The west-bound express rider finally arrived in town. Tad
remembered Graham from the conversation they had before being
interviewed by Mr. Majors. Graham was ready for a rest, big-time!
He, too, had done the work of two riders as they had not secured a
rider at the first home station yet.. He had heard about Tad's fight
with the bandits on the trail. He said one died and the other has a hip
that will never heal right. "At least that is two less bandits the Pony
Express will ever have to worry about," said Graham. "They got what
they deserved!"

Tad bid everyone goodbye as he mounted his next ride. Even
though it was the middle of the night, some of the people from the
local church came out, to send him off. They asked him if they could
pray for him ... and he thanked them very much for their Christian

love and concern. They wished him 'Godspeed', and looked forward to seeing him again on a return trip.

Things went relatively smoothly for a good while, but then one station master said he had heard of a few Paiute Indians that had worked their way farther east than the main tribe, and they were not peaceful. Tad was grateful for the warning, and vowed to be alert at all times ... especially when his visibility was limited. About five miles after one change of horses he saw a couple of Indians ahead on top of a hill off to one side of the trail. They spotted him a second or two later. Both sprinted their horses down hill at an angle to get in front of him. Tad was thinking hard. He didn't want to get in a horse race ... his horse had been running fairly hard for quite a distance already. The Indian's horses may be fresh. The Indians cut down to his path and stopped side by side facing him ... about a hundred yards away. Tad walked his horse slowly toward them. They both put arrows in their bows and pointed them toward him. Tad stopped his horse while still out of range of their arrows. He hollered and motioned for them to get out of the way, knowing it was very probable they may not understand English. They urged their ponies slowly toward him. ... side by side, arrows pointed. Tad is thinking: *the mail must go through ... and so must* **I**! Turning back is not an option. He drew his long-barreled Colt 45, took aim at the Indian on his left, and squeezed the trigger. Bull's eye! The Indian dropped to the ground ... a bullet had caught him right at the base of his neck. The second Indian was so surprised that he shot his arrow at Tad, which came several yards short. He pulled another arrow out of his quiver and started to gallop toward Tad. A second squeeze of the trigger ended the life of this warring Indian also. Tad urged his mount up to the first Indian and dismounted. He took a bracelet and a necklace from him as souvenirs. He dragged both of the Indians' bodies off the trail and behind some bushes in hopes other Indians wouldn't find them and start a big war. Tad got back on his horse all the while thanking God for his protection. He quickly expelled the empty shell casings from his weapon and loaded two more. Now there were five empty bullet holders on his belt. He then urged his horse into a gallop as he knew there was a possibility that additional Indians may have heard the gunfire. Tad was even glad for the eight or ten minutes rest his mount got during the encounter. His horse seemed strong and for that Tad was grateful. His senses were fine-tuned to the possibility of encountering more Indians. Thankfully none appeared, and he safely arrived at the next relay station in Doan's Run, quickly telling the station keeper of his encounter with the Paiutes.

RELAY AND HOME STATIONS came and went. The station keepers all seemed to be good-natured guys. They were always glad to see a rider, warn them of any problems that may lay in the direction they were headed, and quickly hear of any experiences they had before sending them on.

Eventually, Tad ran into his first bad weather. The rain was heavy at times, and Tad was glad his next station was a home station where he could let his clothes dry and get some dry underwear. No allowance had been made for carrying extra clothing; total weight the horse had to carry was top priority. But Tad wasn't complaining ... he would be paid well for these minor inconveniences! And he began more deeply to long to see Laura again ... and plan the future together. He wondered how she would like a bracelet and necklace from a dead Indian! Then he wished he had checked either Indian for a ring ... which could have been her wedding band! He laughed as he rode along. The sky had cleared and the true beauty of the west lay ahead ... and was becoming more and more apparent.

When he reached the home station at Forbes Crossing, he quickly turned the conchila over to the next rider. The mail, as planned so meticulously by Alexander Majors, continued on. Tad wanted to quickly get out of these wet clothes, eat whatever the station tender had available (this time it was baked beans, rice and an apple). It was a good thing there was a lot of beans and rice as he was pretty starved. Now ... to try and get some sleep on a full stomach! He got a good eight hours worth, and then lazily downed some scrambled eggs and toast. Later, Graham showed up with the next conchila. Tad showed him the five empty bullet places on his gun belt. Graham had two himself ... another stray Indian. Tad swung up into the saddle of his next mount and he was on his way again!

TAD FELT HIMSELF very fortunate that this ride was another Rawlings horse ... and he again seemed to recognize Tad. It just gave Tad a little more confidence that if the chips were down and he had to depend on the speed of a horse to escape an undesirable situation ... he had the 'horsepower' under him to do it. Tad took this horse to the next relay station; made the switch in record time. And the next station as well. But the talk of the station tenders was that the Paiute Indians were showing up unexpectedly, and it was best not to push your horse too hard in case it was necessary to call upon it for speed and endurance. The horses the Indians had were not necessarily well fed and cared for ... that being a good thing for Pony Express riders whose owners had bought the best horses they could find.

A couple more home stations, Tad thought. Lessee, that's fourteen more relay stations according to the map, and he would then be at the Brimstone home station ... the farthest west he would be going. Tad was glad. It was hard to believe he will have traveled over six-hundred miles since leaving Tanner. How many days? ... he had lost count

Tad was about halfway to the fifth of six relay stations before Brimstone when he spotted a couple of Indians who saw him and attempted to catch him. This time Tad decided to try to outrun them ... and they gave up the chase after a half mile. He told the station keeper what he had run into, and again made the switch in record time. He pulled into the home station in Brimstone over six-hundred miles behind him ... and then it was heading back to Tanner. Tad was ready for a some 'grub' and 'shuteye' ... as old prospectors and trail-riders called it.

HEADIN' BACK EAST ...

Tad got some good rest and nourishment, as well as conversation with Slim Freeman, the jovial station keeper. In a way, he was somewhat 'saddle-sore', partly due to the lighter weight saddles these horses carried. But, he occasionally had a couple of days layover at a home station which helped. It depended on the frequency of the mail; how the previous riders were able to handle the weather, Indian or bandit problems; relief riders that could not ride due to unexpected sickness, etc. So, all things considered, he felt God was with him every hoof-beat of the journey ... helping him in split-second decisions regarding bandits, and Indians ... whether to stand and fight, or run. He spent much of his saddle time in prayer as he experienced the open plains, beautiful sunrises and sunsets ... and prayer about Laura and the future.

THE EAST-BOUND RIDER, seventeen-year-old Spade Wills, pulled into Brimstone quite exhausted and was so glad to see Tad ready to take over. He had to outrun Indians in two of the last three relays. One horse had taken an arrow in its left flank, but continued to be able to outrun the Indian ponies right into the town of Garver Junction. Spade jumped off his horse, grabbed the mochila and got inside that relay station just as four Paiutes came in behind him. Fortunately he and the station keeper held them off with their guns, the station keeper having a rifle. Three arrows imbedded themselves in the wood front of the relay station, but two dead Indians lay in the street. The other two, one of them wounded, took off the way they came. After a quick drink of water and some beef-jerky, Spade threw the mochila over the fresh horse and continued east. What a story he had to tell his children ... if he lived that long! But he got to Brimstone and Tad wasted no time in throwing the mochila over the saddle of his fresh mount after listening to Spade's tale, and heading east as the sun was setting behind him. He was headed home ... and he prayed for safe travel. Nighttime rides lessened the chance of encountering Indians, and open plains riding was easier than those occasional places of valleys and trees where danger could not be seen much in advance.

Relay station after relay station, home station after home station, and Tad was getting that much closer to Tanner ... and being able to tell his mom and dad, Laura, and Mr. Majors, all the stories he was accumulating.

As he got near where he had shot those two Indians, he wondered if their bodies had been found. He dismounted where he thought they were ... but realized it was still farther on. He walked ahead while holding his horse by the reins, and then recognized the exact spot. The two Paiute bodies were still there ... not looking too good. Tad covered them better with brush and leaves, and paused to say a prayer that the Indians might come to know the God who created them, and who wants them to live in peace with the white-man. Both sides need to work a plan together.

Tad made a quick change at Doan's Run, and then welcomed rest at the home station in Bremming. More relay stations ... then his last home station before Tanner -- Peyton Wells.

Switching horses in Fronter again, he began watching for the place where the bandits had attacked him. He dismounted at the spot, and noticed the rope had been cut ... both ends still tied to the trees. He felt a twinge of guilt that he had not done that himself days ago so that no other rider's horse would trip over it. But he remembered how fearful he was that other bandits could possibly have been lurking nearby, and he needed to get out of there fast. He walked back into the brush into which he had fired and heard that painful yell. No body was there but he could see where a body had been dragged out to the trail. Even bandits must have some sort of friendship with their own kind ... don't they? When Tad got to the relay station in Wardsville, the last relay station before Tanner, he had the surprise of his life!

SURPRISE ...

Tad wondered why Jensen didn't have his next horse saddled and waiting out front. He took the mochila off his horse and went inside the station. And there with Jensen ... was his dad! What an unexpected surprise. They hugged each other, and his dad was sure glad to see his son after his long absence from the family. Jensen just smiled a big tooth-missing grin.

"It's sure good to see you, Tad. You're lookin' great."

"You do too, Dad," said Tad. "I've been thinking about you and Mom a lot these days. Boy, do I have a lot to tell you. But it will have to wait. I've ... I mean 'we' ... have to get this mail on to Tanner. But how are both of us going to ride?"

His dad said, "Follow me."

They went out the door and around to the back stable ... and there were Blitzen and Donner!

"Donner's got a nice full-size comfortable saddle," his dad said. "You'll have to ride Blitzen!" They both got a big laugh out of that. When Blitzen saw Tad, he whinnied and moved his head up and down. "I rode Donner and had Blitzen trail along yesterday. I stayed all night with Bill and Cathy Ward here in Wardsville. They go to our church and make the trip once a month when the weather is good. There isn't a church here in Wardsville, but they host a little Bible study the other three Sundays in their home.

Tad threw the mochila over Blitzen, mounted up, and said to his dad, "Okay, let's **Ride, Cowman, Ride!**" Jensen laughed, but not as hard as Tad and his dad. He obviously didn't get the greater meaning in that statement that the other two did. They thanked Jensen for his good work in supporting the Pony Express, and waved goodbye. Son and dad hit the trail for home.

Jensen was really happy in his job; meeting Pony Express riders; taking healthy care of horses important to the success of this nineteen-hundred mile operation. In the time he spent alone with Porter Rawlings, Porter had told him about the Bible study the Ward's had three weeks out of four. Jensen knew the Wards, and planned to get involved. He said he and his wife needed to learn more about God.

Tad briefly told his dad about some of his experiences but said he would save the details for when they were at home so he could tell his mom also and not have to repeat everything. When he mentioned his run-in with Patch, it reminded him that he needed to pick up Patch's rifle … if it was still there. That was weeks ago that he had stashed it behind a tree. They came upon that area, just before a stream. Tad was pretty sure this was the place. He dismounted and went in three trees, and the rifle was still propped up there. He tied it behind his saddle, and father and son galloped on. Tad asked his dad if he had seen Patch since he left. His dad said that he has seen him in church every Sunday although he didn't get a chance to speak to him. To Tad, that was a good sign.

CONFRONTATION -- OF A NEW KIND ...

Porter took the branch-off trail to Rawlings Ranch, while Tad continued on in toward Tanner a couple of miles ahead. As he slowed to a trot going through town many people smiled and waved to him. Just as he was dismounting Blitzen at the Pony Express station, he heard a familiar "Hey!" ... although it had a slightly different 'ring' to it. He looked around and there was Patch walking quickly toward him ... with a smile on his face! They met at mid-street and Patch put out his hand to shake. Tad did so, as there was a changed look on Patch's face.

Patch told Tad how hard it was for him to get up courage to arrange a meeting with Parson Millard ... but he did. When he asked him what he needed to do to become a Christian, the Parson shared very simply what the Bible said. Patch had never heard the name of Jesus before except when it was taken in vain by his dad. He was awed and truly amazed as the parson explained many of the teachings of Jesus from the New Testament. Side by side, the Parson showed him from the Bible how God had created this earth, and that it wasn't his will that any person miss the opportunity to hear and accept the truth of God's Word on how to receive eternal life.

Slowly and deliberately the parson explained that we all are accountable to God for the sins we have committed in our lives. Patch shuddered to think about the things he had done wrong ... playing tough guy ... being mean to people ... terrible language ... hatred, like he had for Tad.

"I didn't think there was any way that God could accept me because of all that," Patch said. "But then he explained how Jesus had paid for my sins himself, by shedding his blood and dying on the cross. He said my sins were already paid for ... that all I had to do was accept that fact and receive Jesus into my heart as my Lord and Savior. It sounded so simple ... but it was also so clear. The parson went on to say, 'Just as a lifeguard might dive off a pier and swim out to save a drowning person's *body* from a physical death, Jesus' death on the cross saves a person's *soul* from an eternal death.' Parson Millard said we are made up of a body, a soul and a spirit. I never knew that before. But ... I confessed all my sins right there in the parson's office and told God that I accepted what Jesus did for me. I tell ya', Tad ... a huge ... I mean HUGE ... really BIG-time huge ... weight was lifted from my shoulders right then. I ain't ... er, I haven't ... been the same since."

At this point Tad had some tears running down his face as he witnessed right before him, the tremendous change Jesus had made in Patch's heart and life. He almost couldn't believe it! He asked Patch to kneel with him there in the street and pray. Tad didn't feel like he could pray ... he was so choked up at the evidence of such a changed life. So he asked Patch if he could pray, not even knowing if he could do that. But Patch did ... and he thanked God for saving both he and his friend, Tad ... and for making them Christian brothers now instead of enemies. They stood up and hugged each other ... to the applause of those on both sides of the street who had stopped and witnessed this amazing new friendship that God had brought about. What a moment! It was only then that these two young men realized that even horse-pulled wagons and buckboards had stopped in each direction.

Tad and Patch started to part company when Tad said, "Wait!" He ran over to Blitzen and untied Patch's rifle, and took it out to him ... a smile on both of their faces.

Patch accepted it, and as his own tears began to flow, "How close I came to ruining both our lives. Please ... forgive me, Tad."

"No problem on that, Patch ... you're forgiven." They hugged again.

Tad went over to Blitzen, removed the mochila and took it in to Alexander Majors. A great reunion was held in there too. In fact Mr. Majors told Tad that they were having to stop the Pony Express for a while ... hopefully no more than a month ... as they have had to call in the Calvary to put down the Indian uprising. The Paiutes had raided and burned some of the relay stations, stolen many of the horses, been a threat to the riders and, sadly, even killed one ... a fourteen-year-old boy. But that boy took seven Indians with him! Mr. Majors told Tad that he would have to let him know when they would be reinstituting the Pony Express. He said they have been peppered with applicants to be riders for the sheer excitement of the task, so if he decided not to ride any more it would be perfectly okay. ... that there was a girl a few doors down that would like to see him!

After shaking Mr. Majors' hand, Tad took Blitzen's reins and walked a few doors down to Molly's Sewing and Repair Shop. Inside, Laura beamed when she saw Tad. They hugged each other and it seemed like it had been a month of Sundays since they had been together. However, Molly had noticed the buckboards and wagons stopping in the street a little while ago. She had Laura come to the window, and that's when they saw Tad and Patch kneeling in the street with their arms around each other's shoulders. Laura just went into the back room and cried. Life had been quite emotional for her since meeting and falling in love with Tad. Now they both just wanted to pick up where they had left off when Tad had galloped out of town to the cries of *"Ride, cowboy, ride!"*

Tad needed to get back to the ranch, get washed up … thoroughly … and get in some clean clothes. And rest! After a kiss 'good-bye', he made plans to pick up Laura the next day (her mom willingly gave her the day off) for another picnic to the place they had gone before.

Tad, Laura and Molly went outside and saw a small crowd had gathered around Blitzen … this beautiful, cross-cornered-stocking horse that would be the envy of every horse-lover this side of the Missouri River. The other side too! Tad smiled and greeted them. Then he thought, 'How about giving them another exciting take-off.' He backed up several yards, hollered "Aie-e-e-e-e Blitzen," did his running mount catapulting him into the saddle, and Blitzen took off like it was his first leg of the Pony Express … but this time headed toward the Rawlings' Ranch. Several of the town-folk took off their hats and yelled *"Ride, cowboy, ride"* … with big smiles on their faces.

HOME NEVER FELT SO GOOD ... .

MOM WAS SO GLAD to see her son walk in the door. She gave him a good hug in spite of his rather unkempt appearance from who knows how many days on the trail.

"Boy, it sure is good to be back home again, Mom. I really have missed you and dad. Missed your cooking so-o-o-o much! You cook better than any of the station keepers I met! Ha-ha-ha-a-a. Let me get a bath and some clean clothes, and then I will sit down and tell you and dad stories like you've never heard before!"

"Deal," his mom and dad said together ... which caused all three of them to laugh.

TAD COULDN'T GET OVER how great it felt to be in clean clothes and sit in an unbelievably soft, comfortable chair. "I've always appreciated what a nice home God has given us here, but never more than right now."

Tad said, "I've got a present for you, mom," and he pulled out the Indian necklace and bracelet and handed them to her. "It's an Indian necklace and a bracelet. You pick which one you like, and I'll give the other to Laura." His mother looked at both and liked them about the same. She put the bracelet on and was admiring it, when Tad said, "They came off a dead Indian!"

With eyes wide open in amazement, she couldn't get the bracelet off fast enough and hand them both back to Tad. She said, "Are you kidding? No ... No ... I couldn't! Are you joking Tad? Tell me you are."

Tad and Porter both laughed ... and even his dad wanted to know if he was kidding. Instead of answering, Tad went and got his gun belt ... showing them both the five empty bullet holders.

TAD THOUGHT IT WOULD BE a good approach to tell of his experiences ... one bullet at a time! So he did. After he explained each missing bullet, his parent's were left spellbound. Their "little boy" went through all that???

"Dad ... this long-barrel Colt 45 saved my life ... multiple times." Tad was pretty emotional when he explained the confrontation he had with Patch Gaines not long after he left Tanner on the first ride. But even more emotional when he shared about his meeting with him in town just a short time ago. "What an amazing change God has brought into Patch's life."

"Yes," said his dad. "It has been remarkable. I hear he has gone to many people and apologized for the way he had treated them. Parson Millard told me that he has asked Patch to share all about the change God has made in his life with the entire congregation some Sunday soon."

BETWEEN THE BULLETS ...

Tad suggested, "Suppose we eat some good home cookin', and then I will fill you in *between the bullets.*"

"What does that mean?" asked his mom.

"There are a whole lot more experiences that I had besides when I had to protect myself with that super firearm Dad lent me."

"Sounds exciting!" said Lucy. "I'll get something mouth-watering ready in no time."

And his dad said, "Tad, you've earned the right to keep that entire gun-and-belt assembly. It's yours."

"Boy! Thanks, Dad. It means a lot to me. It sure got me out of some tough spots."

After a fine meal that Tad could hardly get enough of, they sat back down in their den and Tad told them story after story *between the bullets* and after: out-running two Indians; having to call on Blitzen to do the job of two horses starting out, and Tad having to do the job of two riders because one broke his leg; riding in the pouring rain; seventeen-year-old Spade Wills being chased by Indians into the relay station, and the standoff he and the station keeper made; hearing from Graham about the results of his run-in with the two bandits; covering up the two Indian bodies on the return trip; riding over the plains at night; and on, and on, and on.

Tad told his mom and dad that Mr. Majors told him that they were having to suspend the Pony Express for a while -- probably a month -- due to the Indian attacks on riders and stations. The U. S. Calvary is expected to make travel safe again by that time. And he told them of one rider, only fourteen years old, who lost his life, but took seven Indians with him.

It was quiet in that den when Tad finished talking ... the three of them letting it all sink in.

"I'm done with the Pony Express," exclaimed Tad. "Mr. Majors said he had more than enough applicants when it starts up again. I really missed you both, and I really missed Laura. I am feeling more and more that it is God's plan for us to spend the rest of our lives together. I don't know if she feels the same way but I am hoping she does. I may find out tomorrow ... we're going on a picnic like we did once before."

Tad's mother wept softly ... so grateful for God keeping her son safe under very dangerous conditions ... and watching God shape and mold her 'boy' into a fine Christian man.

"WE'VE GOT A COUPLE OF MARES out there that are about to foal at any time," Porter said. "We are going to need you, Tad, as we gradually build our numbers up to the 'pre-Majors' days. Monty has had some health problems and the doctor says he needs to cut back on his work for a few weeks."

"I'm lookin' forward to it Dad."

A SPECIAL PICNIC ...

The next day Tad harnessed Donner up to the buckboard, waved good-bye to his mom and dad and headed toward Laura's house. On the way he talked out loud: "How do you ask a girl to marry you? And if you do ... what if she says 'No'? That's kinda' scary. But ... I don't want to be just dating her when I'm an old man! So I'll just pray for God to lead me. Do you hear that, God? Ya' gotta' be there. I can't do this all by myself!"

Tad picked up Laura, and she suggested they go to a new area that had recently been made into a park-like setting. It was right on the banks of the Missouri ... just south of Tanner. Tad felt so good riding along with Laura at his side. He had spent a lot of time alone on the Pony Express trails. He had spent much of that time thinking ... and hoped Laura had too.

They arrived at the picnic area and just sat on a blanket looking over the river. Laura was all smiles, and very talkative. She shared what an amazing thing it was when Patch came into the sewing shop with a smile on his face ... and asked for Laura to forgive him for the way he had been. She readily did so. She knew he was sincere, just by his manner of speaking ... and also having seen him in church regularly. Tad and Laura rejoiced in the change God had made in Patch's life, and decided to pray together for him and his relationship with his father with whom he lived. How wonderful it would be if

Patch could convince his dad that God stood ready to forgive him just like he did Patch.

After their prayer, it got quiet. Neither one spoke for a while as they looked out over the river, and the boats that were going in both directions. It was very peaceful and quiet ... Tad and Laura being the only ones in the area. Finally Tad said, "You know, Laura, I've found that *absence makes the heart grow fonder.*"

Laura looked at Tad and said in amazement, "What a beautiful saying! Where did you hear that?"

"I didn't hear it anywhere. I just thought it, and said it. And it's how I feel about ... us."

Laura replied, "Well I think it's beautiful, and I'm going to remember it ... and tell others. All 'sayings' have to get started somewhere, and I think you've just started one. And ... it's the way I have been feeling ever since you galloped out of Tanner to the cries of *'Ride, cowboy, ride'.*"

Tad said, "Wait here," and he ran up to the buckboard and retrieved a leather pouch. He sat back down next to Laura, opened it and handed her the contents. "It's an Indian necklace and bracelet."

Laura was greatly surprised. She put the necklace around her neck, and the bracelet on her arm.

Tad said, "They are a little big, but I can make them smaller. They came off a dead Indian."

"I know you're kidding, Tad. Did you get them in a town along the Pony Express trail?"

"No. I'm not kidding. It's quite a story. I can tell you how it happened."

Laura quickly took them off, laid them on the blanket and just looked at them ... wondering what the Indian looked like that owned them ... before they were 'stolen'!

She looked at Tad, and neither one knew what to say. Tad kinda' stumbled around in his mind looking for words, and finally said what he thought while out on the trail, "I forgot to see if the Indian had a ring I could give you for a wedding band." ... And then, he could hardly believe he had said that! He quick looked at Laura ... and she was astonished at what he said ... again. She searched his eyes to see if he was really saying what she thought, and hoped, he was saying. Tad got up the nerve to quickly say, "I believe it is God's will for us to get married. What do you think ... God's will is?"

"I think it is too." A kiss and a long hug sealed the deal ... both with big smiles on their faces that neither one could see at the moment. But the smiles stayed there a long time ... as they talked about the future ... and a *real* wedding band!

"I ... I ... don't think I could wear that necklace and bracelet, Tad. I'll have to think about it. Okay?"

"Sure, that's okay," replied Tad. "The more I think about it the stupider it seems to me, too! Maybe we can hang them in our den as decoration. It was a milestone in my life when I had to protect the mail and my own life. It was either him or me. If it had been me ... you would be marrying an Indian!"

They both laughed almost uncontrollably ... for several minutes. Then Laura said, "I have a cousin my age who lives over in St. Joseph. She's coming over to stay with us a week or so. Louise is coming Saturday and will be in church with us Sunday. Now let's get out the lunch. I bet you're starved."

Tad was guilty of 'talking with his mouth full' ... he had so much to tell Laura. He took the same approach he did with his parents: explaining each bullet that was missing in his gun belt, and then 'between the bullets'. Laura just sat amazed as Tad related his experiences. She was relieved when he told her he wasn't going to ride for the Pony Express any more, and that he was going to help his dad as they continued to raise the best horses in the mid-west. They hadn't been able to furnish as many horses to the Calvary and different stagecoach lines since selling so many to Alexander Majors.

The ride back to Laura's house was a happy one. A beautiful future lay ahead of them ... they knew ... because they were placing it in God's hands.

BREAKING THE NEWS …

Pulling the buckboard into the Rawlings' Ranch, Tad saw his mom hanging clothes out on the line to dry. Washing was hard work. Tad went over and put his arms around his mother and told her how much he appreciated all she did in keeping the home going for the three of them. She, in turn, let him know how proud she was of Tad and his father … and that made her work a rewarding task. Tad told her about him and Laura planning to get married. She had to walk over to a stump and sit down and cry … happy tears for them. Tad then left and found his dad out in the corral and told him about the marriage plans. All his dad could say was, "I couldn't be happier for you and Laura, son," and hugged him.

Sunday came and Tad said they better take both the buckboard and the wagon since he probably would be spending some time with Laura and Louise.

As they went into church, Porter and Lucy sat with some friends, and Tad spotted Laura who had saved a place for him. She introduced him to Louise, who was about as pretty as Laura. Tad spotted Patch sitting by himself and motioned for him to come over and sit with them, which he did with a big smile on his face. Patch had never been a necessarily handsome young man, but God had even changed his appearance! Instead of the corners of his mouth turning down, they turned up a little … along with an almost constant smile.

After the sermon was over, Parson Millard announced to the congregation that next Sunday Patch Gaines was going to share with them how God has changed his life. That brought smiles to the faces of everyone present, for they all knew of his former reputation.

Tad agreed to pay for lunch for all four of them -- he, Laura, Louise and Patch -- at The Lucky Rose's Cafe' after church. He made pretty good money for the weeks he was a Pony Express rider. The four of them had a great time together, and their meal dragged out to where they were the last ones to leave. Patch lived close to the restaurant in town, so Tad took Laura and Louise to Laura's house. Louise went inside while Tad and Laura stayed in the buckboard and talked.

Tad said, "I've been thinking about asking Patch to be the best man at our wedding. What do you think?"

"That would be great," replied Laura. "And I think I'll ask Louise to be my maiden of honor."

"Well … we are making progress already" said Laura. "I guess we need to think of at least an approximate date. How does sometime in October seem to you? It's enough time so we won't feel rushed about anything.'

"Sounds good to me," replied Tad. "That is … if tomorrow is too soon for you!" Another time of uncontrollable laughter that shook the buckboard a bit.

THE RIDE BACK TO THE RANCH found Tad more grateful for God's blessings than he had ever felt before … and that was a lot. He and Laura had decided that they would both write down things about their wedding and future life together, so they could talk about them when they were together and not forget anything. Laura's mom had invited Tad over for dinner on Wednesday, so Tad was already looking forward to that.

A PACKED CHURCH ...

Parson Millard, knowing how wide-spread Patch Gaines' reputation was in Tanner, as well as his father's, posted some bulletins in several places in town telling of Patch speaking in church the coming Sunday. When Sunday came, it was the first time the church had ever been absolutely filled to capacity since it started. The parson intentionally gave a short sermon ... so Patch could have the 'last word.'

Patch turned out to be quite a good speaker. He had invited his dad to come, but he had refused. However, as Patch shared from his heart the tremendous turn-around God had made in his life, thanks to Tad Rawlings and Parson Millard, he spotted his father on the very back row ... evidently having come in after the service had started. It caused Patch to stop in mid-sentence for a moment. But he picked up where he was ... just telling his story ... and asking the people present to forgive him if he had hurt any of them. Patch didn't use any notes ... and he didn't leave anything out. He was near tears, however, when he told of the mission he was on -- rifle in hand -- to stop Tad Rawlings dead in his tracks. He told of Tad's accurate shooting that hit the boulder six inches from his hip, and the stone chips that stung his hand. "That will make you pay attention when someone is speaking to you," said Patch ... which brought out laughter from everyone. Except Tad's mother. She was near tears thinking how different the outcome would have been had Tad not spotted Patch's pinto over on the Quarry trail.

When Patch finished there wasn't a dry eye in the church.

Parson Millard dismissed the congregation in prayer, commenting that God had great plans to use Patch in the days ahead … and even speak again in church. Unfortunately, his father left immediately before anyone could speak with him.

Patch was surrounded by new Christian friends, and was still astonished by the difference God had made in his life … and for eternity! As soon as he could get to Tad, he put his arms around him in a strong bear-hug. No doubt this was a friendship that would last a lifetime … and beyond.

Laura's mother and father invited Tad and his parents for dinner after church the following Sunday. Knowing this was Louise's last day with Laura, Tad had driven Old Buster to church with his parents in the wagon. Tad set it up with Laura that every Tuesday afternoon he would come over and they would just take a buckboard ride along the river and talk. Wednesday would be their official 'picnic day', and Friday he would pick her up and bring her back to the ranch for lunch. Tad could also teach her to ride horseback that day. On Sundays would be dinner at the Prescott's, Rawlings's, or the Lucky Rose's. Patch asked Louise if he could take the river ferry over and visit her next Saturday. She seemed very happy for him to. The Prescotts, the Rawlings, and Patch, all said their 'good-byes' to each other after an amazing time at church, which no one who was there will ever forget.

When Porter, Lucy and Tad got back home, Tad's dad told him he wanted to talk with him. So, they went out and sat side by side on the corral fence. His dad asked him if he and Laura had considered where they were going to live after they got married. Tad admitted they had brought it up but came to no conclusion.

Porter said to Tad, "I've got a pretty good offer to make you and Laura on a wedding present from your mom and me."

"What is it, Dad?"

"You and Laura need a home. We've got more acres here than we have ever needed even when we had our maximum number of horses. Do you know where that small clump of trees are on the north border ... about three-fourths of a mile from here?"

Tad thought. "Yes, I know where that is."

Porter continued, "The gentleman your mom and I sit with most Sundays in church, Joel Brand, builds log homes on both sides of the Missouri River. He has a big company, with a great reputation. He's got a couple of signs in town -- maybe you've seen one. They say, 'Build a *Brand* new home.' Sort of a play on words. Mom and I will have Joel's company build a small-to-medium size log home for you and Laura ... three bedrooms. I know he will give us a good price, and maybe even let you do some of the labor. In fact I was wondering if Patch needed a job. Maybe Joel would hire him on to work for him. But ... you would first need to check with Laura and see if this is something she would like. It's important that she not feel obligated to live out here." Porter went on, "Our house is actually over-stocked with furniture, so we can give you some to get you started."

"Wow! You are awesome, Dad. I will ask her about it when we are together next."

Porter continued: "Another thing I might just bring up now -- I haven't spoken with your mom yet. I've wanted someday to get up to where you lived with your biological mother and father when that terrible accident happened. John Rawlings was my brother. I feel bad I haven't been up to see the memorial that was established ... it's just so doggone hard to get away from this horse ranch. As you know there is a lot of work to be done every day. However, if Monty regains his full health, I might be able to hire Patch away from Joel Brand for a short time. Gotta' have honest, reliable help. So I'm thinking that about late next spring, you and Laura might like to join mom and me in taking a trip up there. You came here by stagecoach, but I believe we could upgrade our best wagon, hook two horses to it and make the trip in a shorter length of time than trying to line up stagecoach connections all the way there … maybe cut one-third or more time off the trip both ways. It would be a whole lot cheaper too. The land there belongs to us and I need to decide what to do about that. Probably sell it. Anyway, I thought I'd just bring it up now and we can think about it over the next few months."

"Okay, dad. I believe Laura and I would really look forward to that trip."

WELL, THE SUMMER was drawing to a close, and a lot had taken place. Laura was excited about having a *Brand* new home to begin their marriage. Construction was more than half-way complete on the home. Patch now had a job working for Mr. Brand, and was learning the trade quickly under a Christian foreman, and … on his off-days he was taking his pinto on the Missouri River Ferry and going over to see Louise! Tad spent some time with the home construction when he wasn't working with the horses. One of the two new colts had the cross-cornered stockings which pleased Porter. He didn't want to lose that recessive gene! And more foals were due shortly. (Wade-berry was like dessert for these horses!) Tad had taught Laura how to ride a horse. Mr. Majors assured Tad that the Calvary had quelled the Indian uprising and the Pony Express had started up again. In fact Alexander had Tad address a group of new riders so they could hear about the job 'straight from the horse's mouth'! One Tuesday Tad and Laura took the buckboard, and Tad took her on the first leg of the Pony Express, and into Wardsville. He introduced her to Jensen in the Pony Express station, and invited him to have lunch with them in the local cafe'. On the way back, one of the riders passed Tad and Laura, and when Graham realized it was Tad, he had his horse slow down and ride alongside them as they renewed their acquaintance.

THE BIG DAY ...

Laura's parents surprised the twosome with a week's cruise on the new "Queen of the River" riverboat that was to start its maiden voyage from St. Joseph. It was to take place the week before the date they had set for their wedding, so they moved their wedding date up a week to October fourteenth.

Because of the great impact that the Rawlings family had on the economy of Tanner, on the startup of the Pony Express, on the life of Patch Gaines and undoubtedly many others, Joel Brand was only going to charge Porter for the cost of the materials used for Tad's and Laura's log house ... and even then it would just be the wholesale cost that he had to pay. Joel and his wife were obviously well-to-do, and they generously shared it with the Lord's work as well as with others when the Lord led them to do so.

Well, the big day finally arrived, although for Tad it was too long in coming! They timed everything on their wedding day to coincide with the need to be on the Missouri River Ferry's schedule. It would get them over to the St. Joseph side of the river in plenty of time for the departure of the Queen of the River ... and the beginning of life for Mr. and Mrs. Tad Rawlings.

The wedding went beautifully. Patch had been able to buy some nice clothes from the money he was making at his new job. He looked quite handsome. Louise, likewise, looked every bit the maiden of honor she was ... and then some, in Patch's eyes! But it was tough for any female to compete with the breathtaking beauty of the bride that day. The nicest part about the entire affair, were the well-known personal qualities which God had grown over time in both Tad and Laura. The wedding cake was cut and served in the fellowship room off the main sanctuary. The reception line was moving rather slow; so many wanted to talk to the bride and groom more extensively than their iron-clad schedule would allow. Porter had to make an announcement about the Ferry schedule that the bride and groom had to meet ... and that they will be glad to spend more time in conversation the first Sunday after they returned from their honeymoon.

And so, after a quick change into 'traveling clothes' at church, and along with two suitcases, the bridal party, and many others made the trip to the dock where the ferry would take them across to St. Joseph. They made it in time, and just before they got to St. Joseph, they got a glimpse of the beautiful new Queen of the River ... with cabins and dining area for a week's cruise. What a beauty!

Tad and Laura hugged and kissed everyone goodbye, and boarded the Queen to begin a lifetime honeymoon! Friends and family waved from the shore as the giant paddle wheels churned up the water and the boat moved south. The send-off party also included many from church who had wanted to see this very special event ... like Alexander Majors and his wife, and Joel Brand and his wife.

Patch had his arm around Louise's waist as they waved to Tad and Laura, and in his mind he was thinking ... some day, God. ... please, God ... some day ...

EPILOGUE ...

The discovery of gold in California in 1848 and the onslaught of people moving westward in hopes of striking it rich, made communication between the two coasts a high priority.

The history of the Pony Express is a 'mixed bag.' Different sources have different 'facts' ... primarily due to the onslaught of the Civil War in 1861. No serious attempt was made to preserve an accurate record of riders, rider schedules, etc. In fact there are at least five names suggested to have been the 'first rider' ... six if you want to include Tad Rawlings! Books written contradict each other in many areas. But ... the actuality of this amazing undertaking is secure.

At least sixteen employees were killed (station keepers); hundreds of horses were either run off or stolen by the Indians; many relay stations were burned down ... until U.S. Government forces put down the Indian uprising. The Pony Express shut down for one month, and then picked up right where it left off.

William Cody (later known as Buffalo Bill) helped construct some of the stations as a teenager, and then signed on as a rider. For some reason, he actually rode 322 miles in 21 hours and 40 minutes, using 21 horses. Why? ... The records are not clear, but most likely some teenagers failed to show up to ride when stories of the true dangers began to circulate.

The actual mail came from the east coast to St. Joseph, Missouri only once a week to start. Later, twice a week. (But … that didn't fit the story I wanted to write. Tad had to get back to Laura!) A rider rode approximately eighty miles in a day -- roughly eight hours straight, depending on terrain -- and then ate and bedded down at a home station. So, it appears he may wait another week for the next rider to get there with another "mochila" at which time he would ride another eight hours if "everything worked right." Which … many times it did not. Or he may take the next mochila that came from the opposite direction, and head back the way he came. As I said … setting up these schedules with no 'cell phones' to work with was a huge task. But … they did it, and successfully.

Pony Express riders often passed men installing a cross-country telegraph system … erecting poles and wires. They started simultaneously from the east and west and completed the connection on October 24, 1861. The Pony Express ceased two days later.

It was a great part of our history.

I hope you enjoyed *Ride, Cowboy, Ride*. Being a 'cowboy at heart', I sure enjoyed writing it …

Gordon B. Rose
June 14, 2016
gbrskan54@yahoo.com